RUSE OF HEIRS
A TALES OF RODHLAN NOVEL

HALEY WALDEN

MORAVON PRESS

Ruse of Heirs is an epic fantasy set in a medieval-reminiscent world. Learn more about its themes and tropes at: authorhaleywalden.com/authors-note

ISBN: 979-8-9901106-0-1
(Paperback Edition)

Published by Moravon Press

Developmental Editor: Karie Crawford
Copy Editor: Ashley Olivier
Proofreader: Elyse Grothendick

Cover Illustration by Saint Jupiter
instagram.com/saintjupit3rgr4phic

Map Artist: Cartographybird Maps
cartographybird.com

Author Headshot by Jessica McIntosh Photography
jessicamcintosh.net

BOOKS BY HALEY WALDEN

The Witness Tree Chronicles
1- *Defender of Histories*
1.5- *Ballad of Stallions*
2- *Keeper of Keys*
3- *Vow of Magic*
4- *Sovereign of Clans* (Coming Soon)

Tales of Rodhlan
1- *Ruse of Heirs*

~

Stay up-to-date on bookish news and happenings:
www.authorhaleywalden.com

Follow the author on Instagram, TikTok, and Facebook:
@authorhaleywalden

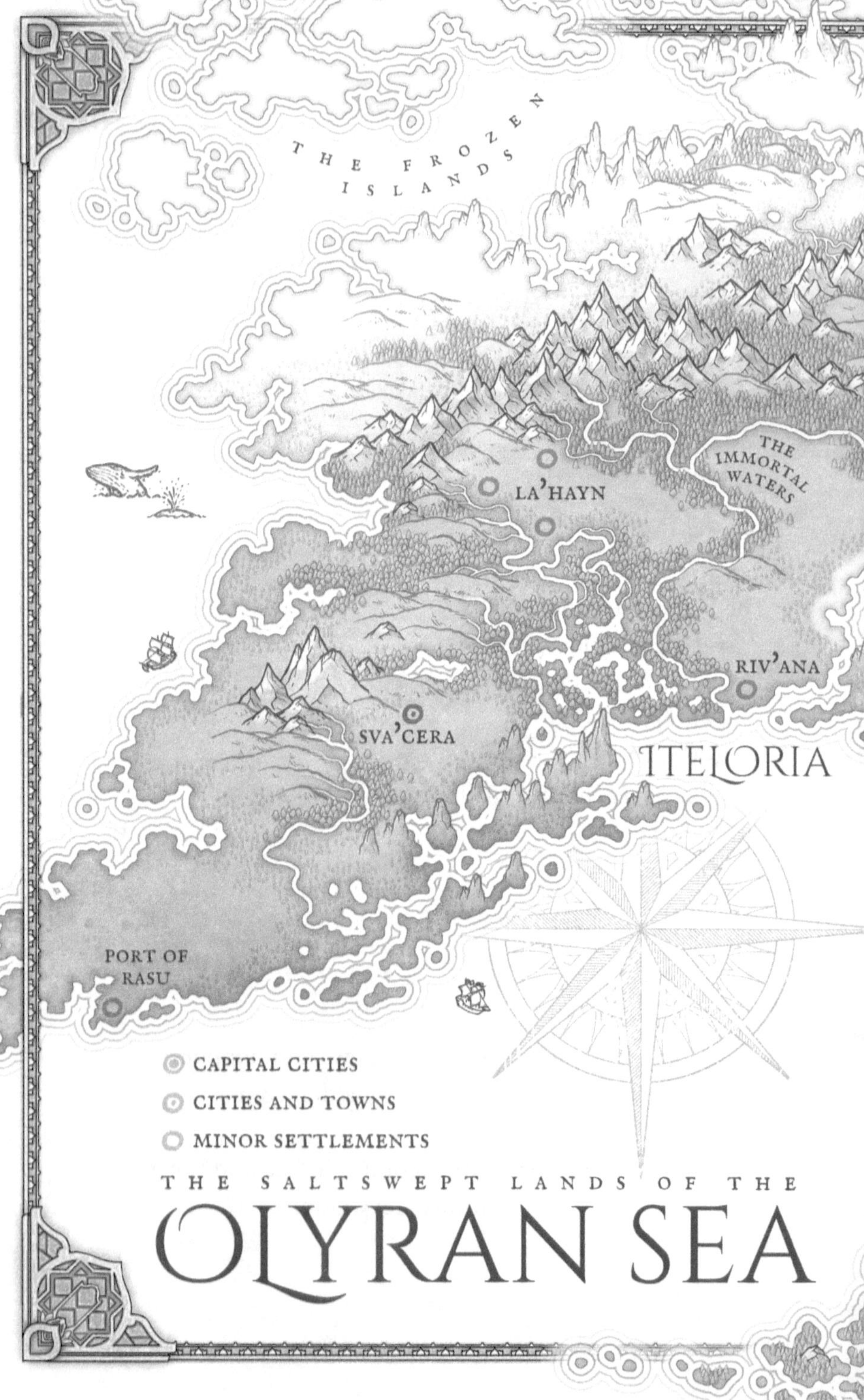

THE FROZEN ISLANDS
THE IMMORTAL WATERS
LA'HAYN
RIV'ANA
SVA'CERA
ITELORIA
PORT OF RASU
CAPITAL CITIES
CITIES AND TOWNS
MINOR SETTLEMENTS
THE SALTSWEPT LANDS OF THE
OLYRAN SEA

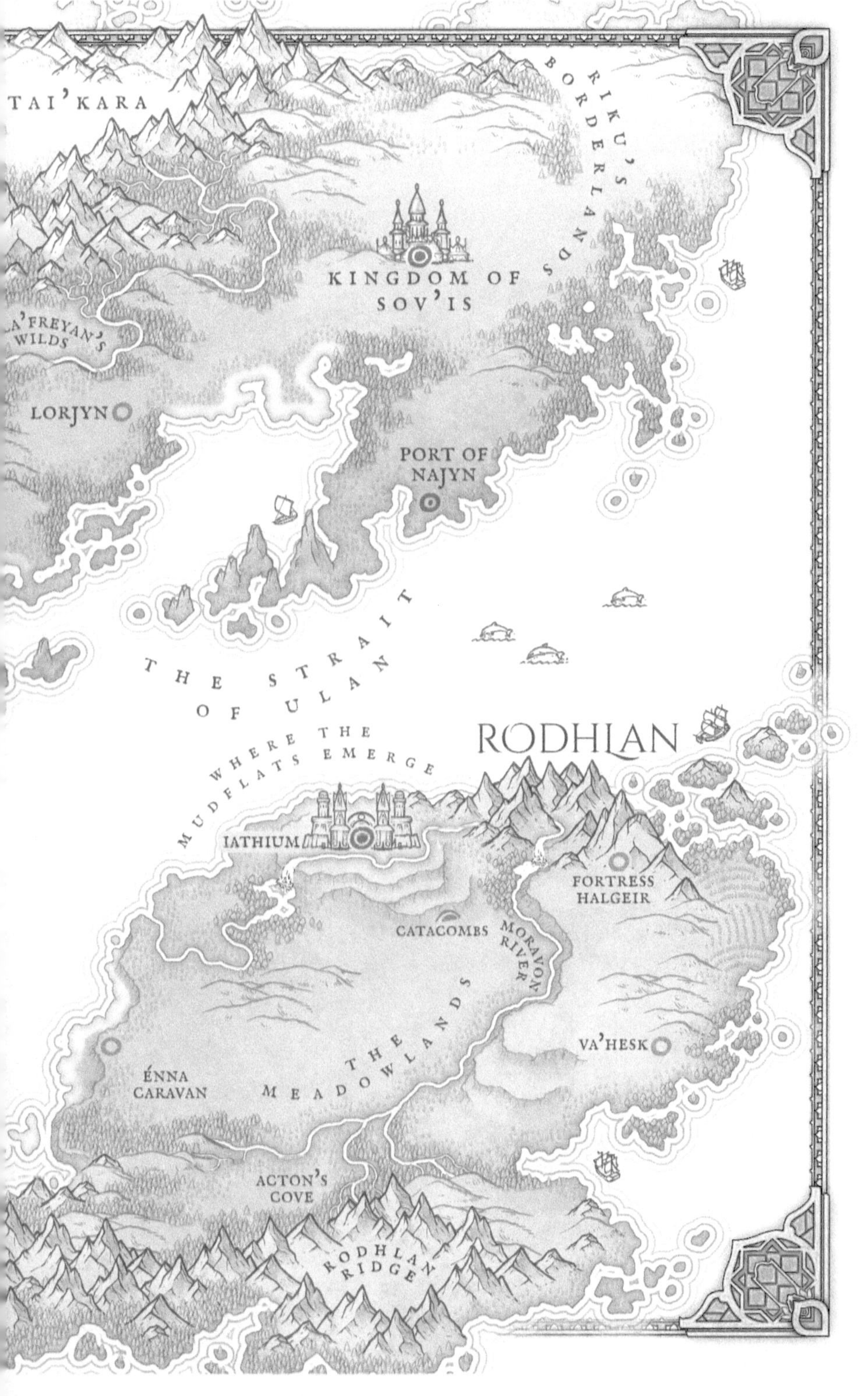

TAI'KARA
RIKU'S BORDERLANDS
KINGDOM OF SOV'IS
LA'FREYAN'S WILDS
LORJYN
PORT OF NAJYN
THE STRAIT OF ULAN
WHERE THE MUDFLATS EMERGE
RODHLAN
IATHIUM
CATACOMBS
MORAVON RIVER
FORTRESS HALGEIR
VA'HESK
ÉNNA CARAVAN
THE MEADOWLANDS
ACTON'S COVE
RODHLAN RIDGE

A Note from the Author

Ruse of Heirs is the first novel in *Tales of Rodhlan*, a series of standalone stories in *The Witness Tree Chronicles* universe.

Ruse takes place 3 years before *Defender of Histories*. It is best read after *Vow of Magic*, but its story stands on its own at any point in the timeline.

Happy reading, my friend!

CHAPTER 1
THORNE BERAN

Thorne Beran braced a large hand against the stone wall before him, his long fingers splayed across its uneven surface as he struggled to control his breathing.

He forced himself to fill his lungs, inhaling through his nose, then holding his breath for eight laborious heartbeats before exhaling. In his open palm, he conjured a weak spark of golden healing magic and pressed it to the center of his chest, desperate for relief.

The dark corridor had always been forgiving at moments like this. Its shadows were the only constant in his life that didn't demand. Didn't scrutinize. Didn't control. Didn't *leave*.

He gritted his teeth and made himself inhale shakily once. Twice. Twice more. A warrior of twenty-one should not require magic or medicine to calm himself.

No, I should be stronger than this. I must be.

Thorne pushed off the wall and straightened his shoulders, exhaling again. This time, the magic he summoned was brighter. Stronger.

When he placed his hand over his heart again, the golden orb sank readily into his skin. His shoulders relaxed, his jaw unclenched, and he sighed, tempted to sink against the cool stone and close his eyes in relief.

But now wasn't the time to rest. His father, Ljós Beran, was returning to the city-state of Iathium again this morning—the ruling seat of their home continent, Rodhlan.

This was Thorne's last chance to tell Ljós the truth: that this might be their final goodbye.

He owed his father that, if nothing else.

The thought made his heart thunder once more, but Thorne shook off the sensation and forced himself to step into the torchlight. He left the shadows' comfort behind and trudged toward his father's chamber.

When Ljós's door came into view, Thorne gave himself one more measure of healing magic. Then, he closed the distance and knocked.

"Enter."

A lump formed in Thorne's throat at the sound of his father's familiar, soothing baritone. It was difficult enough to see Ljós off to Iathium on a normal day. Knowing this might be their last conversation, however, made Thorne's heart ache even more.

With a sweaty palm, Thorne lifted the door's latch and stepped into his father's expansive chamber. Already, Ljós had put out the lanterns. The only light in the large room emanated from a pit of amber stones in the center of the floor. Ljós had illuminated the stones with the golden healing magic of Clan Beran—a birthright both father and son shared.

"*Sjeiva,*" Thorne said gruffly, giving his father a nod.

"My son." Ljós returned the gesture.

The golden magic reflected in his father's dark irises as they regarded one another. Thorne had never resembled Ljós; according to his parents, he looked more like his paternal grandfather. He was larger than his father in both stature and build. To further contrast the physical differences, Ljós kept his hair shorn, while Thorne's thick, blond locks tumbled past his shoulders.

Ljós had never cared for the elaborate hairstyles Clan Beran's men wore, though he kept his beard long and neatly groomed. Thorne had a close-trimmed beard, preferring instead to groom his hair, which he often wove into braids styled after the fabled warriors of their clan.

Thorne's lip curled, tension bunching in his shoulders again.

My son.

He hated the way his father insisted on speaking in Athi. The language was gentle and lilting, with an air of superiority that turned his stomach. It felt wholly foreign in this stone fortress, no matter how often he was forced to listen to it.

"The city's tongue," Thorne replied in Brylla, the language of Clan Beran, forbidden like every other clan language in the land. "Not mine."

"The *lawful* tongue," Ljós shot back, refusing to shift. He raised his chin, sternly holding Thorne's gaze. "You must practice it."

Thorne grunted as he entered the chamber fully, then shut the door behind him.

Ljós was Clan Beran's most gifted healer, yet he had chosen to serve Iathium's Rí, the boy-king Eremon, who seemed to have captured his interest more than anyone or anything in Fortress Halgeir ever had.

Some months ago, Eremon—supreme ruler of Iathium and de facto sovereign of Rodhlan's four clans—had fallen ill under mysterious circumstances. Rumblings of the young ruler's ailment had in turn made their way to Ljós, who had been all too eager to leave Thorne behind to tend to him.

The thought of Ljós doting on the royal brat, rather than

continuing to serve Clan Beran and train its healers, repulsed Thorne. Still, he understood why Ljós had taken the opportunity to flee; Thorne's mother had died the year before, leaving painful memories in her wake. At first, Thorne had hoped Ylanna Beran's death might finally give him an opportunity to grow closer with his father, but his expectations had been thoroughly destroyed.

Thorne shook the thought off, turning his focus back to Eremon and his ailment. Clan Beran's healers quietly speculated that perhaps an enemy of Eremon's had attempted to poison him. Maybe it had even been his own mother, Macha, who controlled her son's every move.

Perhaps, while Ljós had been away, someone had finally succeeded.

Thorne's lip curled in disgust at the thought of the pampered teenager, who was rumored to parade himself through Iathium's fabled Dome wearing brightly-colored silks and preening like some imprudent courtier. Yet he possessed no real political power and seemed content to clash with his council at every opportunity.

What a pathetic excuse for a ruler.

"Why practice Athi?" Thorne retorted, crossing his arms. His gaze drifted to the stones, numbingly taking in their warm and idyllic hues; it was getting harder to look Ljós in the eyes. "We're at home."

"You know the overlord plans to marry a woman with ties to the crown," Ljós answered steadily, though he'd finally relented and shifted into Brylla. "He expects the whole of Clan Beran to protect our ways more diligently. When dignitaries from Iathium visit here, you must be ready to engage them in the common tongue."

Thorne's nostrils flared. One year ago, Artur Beran—the overlord of Clan Beran—had lost his first wife to the fever that had ravaged Fortress Halgeir. It was the same fever that had taken Thorne's mother, driven Ljós to distraction in Iathium, and stoked their ruler's deeply-rooted fear of illness. Artur had lost two of his siblings to River Plague as a boy, and any mention of sickness transformed him from a mighty warrior into a cowering child.

Confusion pinched Thorne's brow. "Is there no suitable bride in Halgeir?"

"There are many, of course," said Ljós. He hefted his leather satchel onto the table by the door, securing its fastenings. "But times are changing quickly, and Artur senses that. It's prudent that he looks to the city for a wife now that he can choose for himself."

Traditionally, Clan Beran's overlords chose wives for their heirs. They were not permitted to marry for love—at least, not on the first match. If an overlord's wife died, he was expected to choose another bride from amongst clan descendants. Someone from within Fortress Halgeir was preferable, of course.

"Hmm." Thorne snorted. "How would a Beran descendant from Iathium adjust to a life here? It can't be done; city-dwellers are weak."

Fortress Halgeir had few comforts to offer, compared to Iathium. The city's eclectic culture blended influences from Rodhlan's four clans, as well as the Itelorian continent across the sea. In contrast, Beran's fortress was isolated, steeped in its own singular heritage, and considered primitive by the city folk.

Beran's people did not enjoy lives of luxury and excess as those in Iathium did, but of strength and hard work instead. Everyone within the fortress had specific responsibilities to keep the clan thriving. Gardeners tended the lush hanging gardens in the courtyard, whose harvests fed the people year-round. In the rolling fields that bordered Fortress Halgeir, farmers tended cattle, sheep, goats, and pigs. Warriors hunted for game in the surrounding meadowlands and beyond, and the animal pelts and furs were used to make bedclothes and winter cloaks.

Collective meals were served in the Arthmael's Hall in the heart of the fortress, where families and warriors alike gathered three times a day. Entire families shared cooking and cleaning tasks on rotation, ensuring everyone did their share.

Healers were trained in Clan Beran's forbidden magic, providing relief to the injured or ill. Long ago, Beran had been widely regarded for its healing powers; now, the magic was used in secret and only among those who had sworn fealty to the overlord.

Although Beran had once been primarily associated with healing magic, it was now most well-known for its powerful warriors. Every member of the clan received some measure of combat training from a young age, and physical strength was of great value. The strongest, most skilled warriors often went on to join the Beravakt, Clan Beran's elite guard, over which Thorne served as general.

"Not Beran." A muscle in his father's jaw twitched. "It is said that Artur courts a descendant of Clan Mór."

Anger erupted in Thorne's gut, its heat racing up his throat and into his face as he clenched his fists at his sides. "*What*?"

This was unheard of. Artur rarely allowed anyone from outside the clan to access the fortress, though when he did, they were forced to swear fealty to Clan Beran. No outsider, especially a city-dweller, had ever ruled here, from on or beside the overlord's throne.

When his father's stoic look didn't waver, Thorne demanded, "How will Artur explain this to the people?"

The questions hung between them, their timbre dense and low.

Ljós and the overlord had always shown unwavering loyalty to Clan Beran. They had inspired Thorne's own pride in his clan. He believed wholeheartedly in the principles they'd taught him since childhood, but now, they'd stooped to adulterating those teachings—to depending on city politics for their very future.

It was abhorrent, and Thorne wouldn't stand for it.

"Artur said he would restore Clan Beran to its former glory," Thorne growled. "I thought that's what we believed in."

Long before the rise of Iathium, Rodhlan had looked to Clan Beran for protection and healing. Fortress Halgeir had once been a place of great influence; its healers, warriors, and overlords had been well respected in ancient times. But then, a mortal god from Iteloria had peacefully conquered Rodhlan, marrying its mother-goddess, Rhona, and tipping the balance of power in his own favor. Over the centuries, the city oppressed the clans, stealing their goddess-given magic and reducing them to chattel.

Some clanspeople had chosen to assimilate into Iathium and capitulate to the city, gaining positions of power at court and making their fortunes by following its rulers. The wisest clan leaders, like Beran's overlord, had self-isolated, strengthening themselves and wielding magic quietly. For many years, Artur had rallied the clan with talk of a return to greater power, wealth, and influence on the continent.

If the overlord was willing to marry *sjivoc*—an outsider— then he had wholly abandoned that dream.

Ljós's expression grew pained, a stark difference from the mask of calm and steadiness that he typically held. "Times have changed," he answered in Brylla, lowering his voice. "We must do what is necessary."

His gentle tone stoked Thorne's ire more. "You find it necessary for the overlord to invite outsiders into our home?"

"He has little choice."

Thorne could feel his heart beginning to pound like it had in the corridor. "No one escapes that city unstained."

"If you knew what the Rí intended," Ljós said, "you wouldn't be so headstrong."

"The boy-king is a curse all on his own," Thorne spat. "I had hoped his influence would end with you, but now he has poisoned Artur's mind, and he used you to do it."

Ljós shook his head, raising a hand as if to calm his son. "If you understood the overlord's reasoning—"

Thorne cut his father off, raising his voice. "I will soon enough." His nostrils flared, his ears burning as he added, "When I win the trials, I'll have the right to know everything he does."

There it was: the truth Thorne had been unable to utter in the precious few days Ljós had spent back home. He had reluctantly joined the Arthmael's Trials, a grueling test of strength and fortitude meant to select Clan Beran's next Anointed heir.

His father paled, recoiling. "You'll do no such thing. We had a covenant."

Thorne set his jaw, trying to ignore the hurt in Ljós's eyes. "We agreed I would not pursue the throne for *sjeima*'s benefit." His mother. "But she's dead now. This is not for her sake; it's for mine."

"Ylanna meant to use you for influence, but you've never wanted the throne." It was clear Ljós was incapable of hiding the desperation in his voice. He took a step closer, and his next words wavered when he spoke again. "She never forgave me for following our fathers' wishes, for marrying her and staunching her ambitions."

"This isn't about influence," Thorne answered quickly, trying to ignore the pang of hurt that tightened his stomach. His father was becoming too honest. Too soft. "It's about strength."

Ljós shook his head slowly, closing his eyes. "You have nothing more to prove."

"Clan Beran is weakening." Thorne crossed his bare arms, the movement creating uncomfortable friction against his fitted leather tunic. "With the right heir, it could become strong again. The people deserve to be protected."

The heir would assume the title of overlord when Artur died or stepped aside. According to legend, the clans' Anointed had once inherited an extra measure of ancestral magic that set them aside from their peers and gave them a place of authority at the head of their clan. Here in Fortress Halgeir, the anointing amounted to a throne, and Thorne had set his sights on it.

"One perceives weakness when one lacks understanding," Ljós said sadly. "If you've entered the trials, as you say, your decision cannot be taken back."

Not without dire consequences of some sort: loss of reputation, exile, loss of life. The results lay in Artur's hands alone.

"No," Thorne replied, raising his chin. "It can't."

"You *will* prove your strength. I don't doubt that," his father continued. Anger began to cloud his features. "But you've given up your freedom in exchange for it."

"No one in Rodhlan is free, least of all the clans," snapped Thorne. "I have chosen my side."

"Then there's nothing more to say." Ljós leveled a hard look at his son before shouldering his healer's satchel. In smooth Athi, he said, "I wish you well, but I must return to Iathium."

"To your Rí."

"Yes," his father said, moving toward the door, "and yours. There may come a time when the *boy-king* reclaims his true power and demands your respect. And you'll give that to him, if you truly want Clan Beran to survive."

By now, Thorne's body was trembling with rage. How dare his father speak such treason in Artur's fortress?

"Beran will stand on its own without the city. And if Artur does not see to it, then I will," Thorne warned, voice low.

Ljós unlatched the door, pulling it open. Before he stepped out, he sighed heavily.

"This is what your mother wanted, a warmongering son," he said, his voice taking on a harsh edge that grated against Thorne. "Perhaps in death, she will finally be satisfied."

ODA BERAN

"How long will you be at the coast, Mum?" Oda Beran applied a honey poultice to the shallow wound on her sister's shoulder, her eyes on her work and her ears attuned to her mother's answer.

"Eight weeks, at best. I won't return until summer solstice or after, and that all depends on your uncle's recovery," said their mother, Elda, who worked on the opposite side of the family's dwelling chamber. "You still have time to change your minds—both of you. I want you with me on the journey."

From behind her, Oda could hear soft rustling and the padding of Elda's leather boots as her mother moved about, packing her belongings. Elda was preparing to travel to Clan Énna's settlement on the western coast of Rodhlan, as she did every spring. This was the first year she would go without either of her daughters, and the third time she'd made the long trip since their father's death.

There was a sense of urgency around Elda's visit this year; Rune, their father's youngest brother, was gravely ill, his body riddled with infection. Oda's grandmother had sent for Elda, begging for aid. Now, their cozy, candlelit chamber smelled strongly of the herbs, poultices, and balms Elda had prepared for Rune's treatment.

"You know we would come with you, if it weren't for the uncertainty," Oda answered, brow furrowing as she conjured a golden orb of healing magic to apply to Cynda's wound. "We don't know when you'll be able to return. And then, there's the matter of the Arthmael's Trials."

Her mother made a disapproving noise at the back of her throat. If Oda had been at liberty to turn her attention to Elda, she knew she would have seen a glare that matched the sound. Bright green eyes, contrasted against dark brown skin, would be piercing a hole directly through Oda's very soul. She could feel the sting of that scrutiny enough, as it was.

"If I could force my will, I would have both of you by my side to see this through. Anywhere but here," Elda answered in a low voice, moving nearer to the young women.

"I would come with you, if Oda weren't so stubborn," said her older sister, Cynda. She shifted on the bed where she sat, and Oda stopped the flow of her healing magic, raising her hands.

"Be still," Oda chided softly. "I'm almost finished."

Cynda obeyed, then continued pointedly. "But since she insists on serving as a healer *and* among the Beravakt, someone has to look after her."

Oda had been accepted into the ranks of Clan Beran's elite guard only two years ago. For a sixteen-year-old outsider whose father was a descendant of Clan Énna, that had been both a rarity and an incredible honor. Though she and her family had the freedom to come and go from Fortress Halgeir as they wished, she was reluctant to leave—especially not knowing how long their journey would be. Cynda had accompanied Elda every year until now.

"You could go," Oda suggested, biting her lip in frustration as she applied a final layer of poultice and reached for clean bandages. She had closed the wound without a single stitch, but the site could still scar if not properly treated. "I don't need anyone looking out for me."

"The trials have been known to mark the beginning of blood feuds between competitors," Elda retorted. "You'll need to be on alert."

However many manage to survive, Oda thought with a grimace. The impending trials had made their mother uncharacteristically nervous.

Oda carefully pressed a strip of linen bandage to the cut, her heart beating a little faster at her mother's words, though it was best not to reply. Cynda stiffened, hissing as Oda bound the injury.

"That hurts," Cynda whined.

"Hold still, or you'll make it worse." Oda answered firmly. "And this is the only time I get to order you about, so let me enjoy it."

Cynda groaned. "If you weren't so good at this, I would demand a different healer. But she who inflicted the cut must now bind it."

Oda snorted, stepping back to survey her work. "Keep your footing in the ring next time, and maybe I won't slice you."

The sisters had been sparring in the arena when Cynda had stumbled. Although Oda always kept impeccable control of her blade, accidents were inevitable. Thankfully, she'd been able to minimize the damage, and the cut her sister sustained would heal quickly.

Cynda stood, rolling her shoulders and stretching her neck before turning to grin at Oda. At twenty, she stood taller and slimmer than her sister, a picture of grace with her willowy figure, brown eyes, and long black braids. Aside from the wound, Cynda looked more like a dancer than a fighter. Perhaps if they'd moved to Iathium instead of their mother's home territory, Cynda might have taken up dance instead of working in the overlord's hanging gardens. Performers were revered in the city and were often wealthy. Rather than reading books to whet their appetite for stories of the past, city-dwellers paid richly for song, dance, art, and theatrical performances.

Oda helped Cynda slip into a long, loose blue tunic that covered her bandages. The fitted one she'd worn in the ring was now ruined and bloodstained. She wasn't sure whether it could be salvaged, but she would try to clean and repair the soft, thin wool.

In contrast to Cynda, Oda was shorter and more muscular, with generous curves she had learned to accept as she grew into adulthood. She was still clad in her boots, training leggings, and the sleeveless leather tunic she preferred for ease of movement in the arena. Her black curls were arranged into twists that fell past her shoulders, which she often gathered at her nape with a thin leather cord for training.

Elda stepped closer and grasped Cynda's hand, keeping her firm eyes trained on Oda. "I know what you're doing, changing the topic. Refusing to answer. But before I go, you'll listen to me."

"You have nothing to fear, Mum," Cynda said soothingly, squeezing their mother's hand in reassurance.

"I'm not worried for myself, and you know it. I heard stories of Artur's trials, of the families who fought over the throne, the blood that was spilled afterward. And it's worse."

Oda rolled her eyes and sighed, but Elda struck out to grasp her arm, her fingers digging in.

"Don't make light of this, Oda," she said through gritted teeth. "There is the heir's betrothal to consider."

Ah. Oda had forgotten about that particular tradition. Artur would select a wife for the trials' winner, and he would choose whomever he deemed most loyal to Clan Beran. That meant outsiders like Oda and Cynda would be unfit for consideration.

"We're half Énna," Oda replied, wrinkling her nose. "Artur

will want a true Beran descendant for his heir; you don't have to worry about us."

"Whatever happens, this is a dangerous time for the entire clan," Elda protested. "I'm asking you once more: Will you come with me?"

The desperation in her voice, her pained expression, made Oda's heart squeeze. She exchanged a glance with her sister, who merely shook her head and gave their mother a gentle smile.

"I'm going to stay with Oda," Cynda said carefully, "though I wish I could be in both places at once."

"I have to keep my rank," Oda added, fighting the urge to apologize. "The moment I'm able, I'll come to visit Rune. You have my word, and you can tell him so."

Oda had been treated like an outsider here for most of her life, although she had lived with Clan Beran since she was a small child. Her acceptance among the Beravakt warriors had been hard-won, and she still often felt like she was teetering on the edge of being ostracized once again. She couldn't afford to disappear from the fortress now, especially during the trials. But once the overlord's heir had been chosen, she would feel safer taking some time away.

Besides, she was close to winning favor with Thorne, the youngest general to ever lead the Beravakt. If she earned the right to train with the competitors, as they would all need sparring partners who were not part of the trials, then she could further prove herself.

Her combat skills were already fine-tuned, and her expertise with a blade was unmatched among many of Clan Beran's best fighters.

Elda closed her eyes and sighed sadly. "Then I've done all I can."

There was a knock at the chamber door, which jolted Elda to alertness. Cynda crossed the room to open it, peering out.

"Enter," she said and took a step back.

Morning light streamed in around Thorne's towering silhouette. Instantly, Oda was on alert. She stood up straighter, shoulders back, almost as though at attention.

But Thorne's attention was solely fixed on Elda, who was shrugging a brown, fur-lined traveling cloak over her green tunic. She gathered her satchel and turned to him.

"My father is ready," Thorne said, not bothering to step inside the chamber. He wore leather breeches and a long-sleeved tunic of rough-spun gray wool, and he had pulled his hair out of his face. Loose tresses and braids fell over his shoulders, and his beard was neatly trimmed. "He can take you as far as Iathium's gates, and you'll be able to charter a horse and cart from there."

"Will it only be Mum and Ljós?" Cynda asked, casting a worried glance toward Elda.

"Two of my warriors will go with them," Thorne answered. "They'll be safe."

"Thank you," Oda said, visibly relieved.

The words sounded thin and weak—*nervous*—as they left her lips, and her cheeks grew hot. She wished she had said nothing at all.

Oda wasn't accustomed to interacting with the general in her family's home. Normally, their rapport was much more relaxed, even somewhat friendly. It shouldn't have made such a difference to have him standing at her front door, but it did.

Thorne glanced in her direction and gave her a nod. His warm amber eyes glinted in the chamber's torchlight before falling to the table where she'd spread out her healer's implements. Concern flashed across his expression, subtle and fleeting, but there all the same.

"Is someone hurt?" he asked.

Oda jerked her chin in her sister's direction. "Sparring accident."

"Oda patched me up," Cynda answered with a shrug.

He hummed a guttural, "Hmm," then looked back to Elda, extending his hand. "Your things?"

Elda handed her traveling satchel to Thorne, who slung it over his broad shoulder as though it weighed nothing. "I'll take this down to the boat and come back for you."

He ducked back out the door, and Oda felt herself relax.

Cynda embraced Elda first, kissing her cheeks. "I love you, Mum. We're going to be all right."

"And give Uncle Rune our best," Oda added, stepping forward to embrace Elda.

"I will," Elda said into her hair, squeezing her hard. "I often wonder what might have become of us if we'd stayed with your father's clan."

Oda tightened her own grip on her mother's smaller frame. Elda's sorrow was palpable, but it made no sense. She and Oda's father, Uden, had worked hard to gain a place among Beran's people. They had even taken Beran's clan surname, swearing fealty to Artur and abandoning the wandering life they'd once known among Énna's nomadic people.

"I have to meet Reyne and Jund at the gardens," Cynda murmured, breaking through Oda's racing thoughts. She gave their mother one last peck on the cheek and headed toward the chamber door. "Safe travels, *sjeima*."

As soon as Cynda left the room, Elda grasped Oda's face, wide-eyed. A frantic stream of whispers poured from her lips, so quickly that Oda almost couldn't understand her words.

"Listen closely, Oda. Artur promised your father—he *promised*," Elda said, voice nearly inaudible. Her mother's entire body was trembling. "It was part of their agreement."

Oda had once heard her parents whisper of a deal her father had struck with Artur long ago, but she had never asked questions about it. Her heartbeat pounded in her ears.

"What agreement?" Oda whispered. "What did he promise?"

"To keep our family uninvolved." Elda paused, her hands dropping to Oda's shoulders as she tilted her head, obviously listening for Thorne's return. When she was satisfied the coast was clear, she continued. "Listen carefully.

"Artur will choose seven women for his heir. Only one will marry the winner of the trials, but all seven will be sent away from Fortress Halgeir for five years afterward. No one is to know the true bride until the end of that five years."

A cold shiver swept across Oda's skin, and she swore under her breath, earning a disapproving look from Elda. "*What*?"

"Quiet!" Elda raised a finger to her lips, watching the door for another moment before she continued. "It's the heir's final trial. He must show full submission to the overlord by willingly giving up his bride after the wedding night. Once the five years have passed, she can return to share his bed again—on one condition. The heir must not break trust by betraying her identity. If he does, they will both be put to death."

Oda's lip curled in disgust. "That's cruel."

Elda nodded. "Cruel to all involved. The girls' families can't know where their daughters have been sent; they must trust in the overlord's protection or risk death as well. And during that time, those daughters may not choose a life for themselves, much less a partner. It's a test of loyalty and trust for everyone in the clan."

Oda could see why her parents would have bargained with Artur to keep them out of the selection. The thought of seven daughters being taken from seven families and hidden away for five years stoked hot rage within her. She had never loved Clan Beran's overlord, but now, she thought she might truly hate him.

Curling her fingers into fists, she said, "I knew Artur was overbearing, but this—"

"Say nothing more, if you want to protect our family." Elda

pulled Oda into one last embrace. "I only wish you would come with me. I'm afraid for you both."

"If Papa and Artur had an agreement, I'm sure we'll be fine," Oda replied, smoothing a hand over her mother's graying hair. Doubt coated her words, and they stuck in her throat. "Clan loyalty wins the day in this place. He'll choose women with seven or eight generations of forefathers hailing from Fortress Halgeir; we likely have nothing to fear."

Elda smiled sadly, tears glistening in her eyes, a mirror of Oda's own. "For all our sakes, I hope you're right."

CHAPTER 3

THORNE

It was midday by the time Thorne made it to the arena for training. He'd seen off his father and one of the senior healers, Elda, who was traveling to the western coast for an undetermined period of time.

Losing two of Clan Beran's best and most experienced healers during the trials was a risk, but they trusted their apprentices were up to the task.

Thorne wasn't so sure.

As a healer's apprentice himself, Thorne could assist with binding some wounds. But he had never developed any significant skill in the arts of mending muscle, bone, or tissue. At best, he could bind a wound until a more skilled healer could assess it. He seemed to be more well-versed in addressing emotional ailments rather than physical ones.

He stepped into the expansive stone arena, which had been carved out of the craggy mountainside like the rest of Fortress Halgeir. As he descended the wide steps toward the training floor, he felt his breath catch, and he wished that he had used more of that magic to calm himself before coming here. Already, women and children were decorating the upper perimeter of the arena for next week's trials, stringing garlands of linen and vine around the vast, torchlit chamber.

The training floor below, where he had spent much of his time since coming of age, would transform into a battleground in the days ahead. Artur had held his throne for thirty years before deigning to choose an heir, but it was time. Murmurings amongst the clan had betrayed the people's uncertainty about his delays, but that wariness had finally transformed into a hopeful sense of anticipation.

Thorne tried to shake off the growing sense of dread in his chest. He'd thought the feeling might be relieved once he told his father he intended to compete. But now he wondered whether he had simply made the wrong decision to enter the trials in the first place.

No, he told himself. *Tyr is too boastful, and Mund is a coward with brute strength. Anj is too old, and Nyft is too weak. I can offer hope to the clan that these men can't. There's no choice but to push ahead, for the good of Beran.*

"Are you in there?"

Thorne blinked, bringing his awareness to the present. Oda stood before him, arms crossed, her full lips twisted into a bemused smirk. He'd gotten so lost in his thoughts that he'd reached the training floor without realizing it.

He narrowed his eyes. "Where else?"

There was something behind her hard stare he couldn't quite place; frustration, perhaps? Irritation? Whatever it was, it had taken very little effort to stoke. An accomplishment either way, he decided. Most days, it took much more than two words to rile her.

It was tempting to smile, but as General of the Beravakt, amusement was a luxury Thorne couldn't afford to partake in. At least, not in the arena, and not where women and children might see. Artur expected his warriors' countenances to reflect the seriousness of their duties: protecting the clan, upholding justice within the fortress's walls, and making an example of those who refused to comply.

"You looked vacant," she answered, turning to saunter further onto the training floor. "Like your spirit sent your body here while it went on an adventure."

He snorted and followed, observing each subtle shift in her form as she walked. Each movement was smoother than the calm waters of Acton's Cove near Rodhlan's southern mountain range. Her fighting style echoed the same steady assurance, the picture of grace and power.

The female warriors he'd trained with over the years had always fascinated him in that way, and he particularly enjoyed trying to emulate their level of skill and restraint. So many of his men moved in bursts of power and sheer force, tiring quickly as a result. On the other hand, the female Beravakt carefully preserved their energy, resulting in unmatched stamina and poise in combat.

Long ago, Thorne had decided it was infinitely more satisfying to spar with a woman than to do battle with a man. Maybe he could use those observations to his advantage during the trials.

When they reached their preferred training circle on the ring's far side, Oda drew her axe, flipping it in one hand. Her hair swayed around her face as she sank into a fighting stance. In response, Thorne drew his broadsword.

"Thank you for helping Mum," she said, taking the first lunge.

Thorne blocked her strike with his blade and deflected the axe. Her use of the common Énna endearment for *mother* had always made him feel uneasy, but he had overlooked it before.

Now, he thought about Artur's fraternizing with an outsider —and the dangers of diluting clan loyalty that came with it. He scowled, launching a counterattack.

"Why don't you call her *sjeima*?" he asked. "She was born of Beran."

Oda's hard block reverberated up his blade. "Papa called her Mum. She prefers it."

After everything Oda's family had done to assimilate here, it seemed silly that they would insist on using Athi terms. "Beran's ways are more respectful."

Her eyes darkened with rage as she drew back and lowered her axe. "I do *not* disrespect my kin in word or deed. Especially not her."

Thorne threw a pointed look at her weapon. "Back in position," he barked.

She threw it to the ground instead, unsheathing her own broadsword, which she'd been carrying on her back. "Explain your insult."

"It's not an insult; it's the truth," he said, assuming his fighting stance. "Unwavering loyalty makes us strong."

"Compassionate leaders earn loyalty," she challenged. "Cruelty erodes it."

Brandishing the blade, she lunged at him, her sword's tip slicing just a breadth away from his chest. He blocked, parried, counterattacked. Steel clashed against steel as Oda moved with relentless fury, faster than he'd ever seen her fight before.

"Strength demands cruelty," Thorne said, trying to steady his breathing as he swung again. "The people follow strength."

"Because they're afraid not to. So, answer me this." She blocked his next strike before continuing. Beads of sweat rolled down her forehead, her chest rapidly rising and falling. "Does a stronger clan emerge from true loyalty, or from fearful submission?"

Parry. Strike. Block. Counterstrike.

She challenged, "What force makes a warrior's heart beat in time with her brothers'? Is it the erratic pulse of fear, or the steady drum of love?"

Thorne wasn't willing to answer that, nor could he allow Oda the upper hand. Not when this clan would soon look to him as their next overlord.

"A leader can't afford to crave love," he replied. "Not the overlord, and not his heir."

"Then we're doomed," said Oda, striking again, "because they will never know true loyalty."

"When I am heir, you'll see it can be done," snapped Thorne.

"You entered the trials?" Oda scoffed, her voice tinged with bitterness. "I thought better of you than that. Maybe I was wrong."

A flash of confusion muddled Thorne's thoughts. Why would Oda think less of him for entering the trials? Furthermore, why should he care what she thought about it? He'd done what he felt he must. That was enough.

Their blades locked, and they drove hard against one another, their opposing forces creating a deadly balance. One misstep, one stumble, and one would emerge the victor. Thorne thrust a burst of energy against Oda's sword, but she held firm.

"Yield," he growled, pressing firmer with his sword.

"*You* yield," she replied through gritted teeth.

Angry heat crept up his neck and into his face. "Not today, *sjivoc*," he spat.

Outsider.

The word had its desired effect. Oda's eyes went wide, and she yielded just enough to give Thorne the momentum he wanted. He was going to end this match before she got the better of him in the presence of his people.

"An heir must be strong."

The memory of his mother's voice echoed through his mind, drawing his attention away from his blade. He sucked in a breath, his mind clouding as his heartbeat quickened.

In that same moment, Oda dodged his clumsy, heavy-handed strike, disarming him as she drove her boot into the back of his knee. He crashed to the arena floor at the same moment his sword clattered onto the packed dirt, catching himself on his knees and palms. His hands stung from the impact, which then reverberated up his arms and into his shoulders.

The arena fell silent as Oda strode over to where his sword had fallen, then gave it a mighty kick. She stomped off the training floor without another word.

"But you are not strong. You will never be strong."

Ylanna's rich, taunting voice was just as clear as it had been before she died—and just as scathing.

Quiet, he silently raged.

Thorne forced himself to rise. Trained his expression into impassivity as he took several long, painful strides to collect his sword. Moved toward the steps and began to climb.

The people's eyes were on him; he could feel it. Truly, they should be impressed with Oda's skill. After all, Thorne had been a part of her training. She was this strong and capable, in part, because of him. If nothing else, they could see how furious his fighters truly were.

Couldn't they?

Thorne picked up his pace, exiting the arena at a clip and heading toward his father's chambers. His mother's memory gripped his throat, hindering his ability to draw a full breath. Panic seized his chest as he sheathed his sword and moved purposefully down the long stone corridor.

"No one cares for a weak boy. He dies alone in the wilderness because he cannot fend for himself." Ylanna had often reminded Thorne of his fragility as a child. Had it not been for Ljós, Thorne wouldn't have survived infancy. *"Only the strong are worthy. Only the strong are loved. You are neither, nor will you ever be."*

Time and again, his father had reminded him that her words were carefully placed to coerce specific actions. In truth, Ylanna had recognized Thorne's strength and talent for fighting. She knew he was capable of making a bid for the throne, but he had not wanted power when he was young. And after she'd died, he'd felt selfishly relieved, knowing he would no longer have to endure her cruelty.

He had expected her voice to fade into nothing now that she was gone, but instead, it had only grown stronger. Haunting him in moments like these.

Moments of failure.

Thorne had spent his life trying to prove his mother's words wrong.

He had risen to the rank of general and was one of Artur's most skilled fighters. Time and again, he had achieved everything he'd set his mind to. But no matter what he accomplished, Ylanna's words still reverberated through his head.

Maybe once he won the trials, she would finally be silenced.

CHAPTER 4
ODA

Oda frantically gathered her belongings, stuffing a change of clothing and a fresh bar of soap into her burlap rucksack.

She rummaged through the chamber she shared with her sister, assessing what items would serve them best on their journey. Opening a second sack, she rolled trousers and tunics into a bundle, then stuffed them inside as well.

Cynda had said she was only staying at Fortress Halgeir because of Oda. Perhaps if Oda left for the western coast now, her sister would follow. If they left by late afternoon, they could make it to the meadowlands before nightfall. And if they used the small bit of coin Elda had left for them, they could charter horses south of Iathium and catch up with her more quickly.

Her mother's words about the trials, about their father's deal with Artur, had disturbed her more deeply than she cared to admit. If she and her sister weren't here when Artur chose suitors for his heir, then he couldn't select either of them.

That had been Elda's motivation all along. Leaving for Rune's sake had simply been a conveniently-timed excuse.

In the end, Elda had allowed her daughters to make their

own decisions, as she always did. For Oda's entire life, the deepest lessons had always been found in those choices, right or wrong.

But this time, Oda feared their decision might have been the wrong one. She had seen it in her mother's dark, fearful eyes.

Equally daunting was the question of how Thorne might retaliate for her insolence in the arena. He'd shown his hand, and she had shown hers. After humiliating him the way she had, she would never rise any higher in the ranks. In fact, she might be demoted or driven out completely.

After everything she'd sacrificed, this would be the end for her. She would be better off going to live with Rune for a while. Perhaps Clan Énna's night patrol could use an extra blade. If worst came to worst, she could go to Iathium and join the sentries.

She shuddered at the thought. *At least the Rí doesn't terrorize young women and their families.*

On the contrary, he seemed to do the opposite.

She'd heard rumors making the rounds that a cousin of hers, a young courtier in Iathium, was close with Eremon. Maybe she could convince her family to take her in, get her acquainted with the sentries' commanders.

The thought of living in Iathium, of all places, was loathsome. But it didn't compare to the brutality that was about to take place here.

Oda had foolishly believed that she and Thorne had built a rapport. They had trained side-by-side daily, and she had even begun to think of him as a friend. Why had he felt the need to remind her just how much of an outsider she still was?

"Not today, sjivoc."

"Not today, you heartless brute," she muttered angrily.

Oda left the rucksacks on her bed and entered her mother's sleeping quarters, where she kept her healer's implements. She opened the ornate wooden box where Elda stored her tinctures and powders. Drawing out a few empty glass bottles, she stowed the rest away again and rose.

Her story was already prepared: Elda had forgotten two of her most crucial remedies, and it was imperative that Oda and Cynda take them to her. Their uncle's survival depended on it.

Oda would fill the bottles with supplies from Ljós's chamber, then notify Thorne that she and her sister would be accompanying their mother after all. That would be that. There was no need for them to make themselves vulnerable to this clan's cruelty; they were old enough to pave their own way in the world now.

If she was truly an outsider in Thorne's eyes, then she would never really be accepted here. And when he won the title of Anointed—because there was no doubt he would—that alone would seal her fate. Oda wasn't willing to continue fighting for an unattainable future.

She emerged into the stone corridor with purpose, walking through alternating shafts of shadow and bright midday sunlight as she descended the wide, winding path that led to the healer's chambers. Fortress Halgeir was truly magnificent: a spiraling stone fortress built into northern Rodhlan's natural landscape, with intricate pathways, hanging gardens, and hundreds of hidden living quarters.

No other place on the continent possessed the advanced technologies Beran did, either. Oda was aware her father had helped Artur to engineer running water for every chamber, likely using the water magic he'd inherited from Clan Énna. She had never personally witnessed such power, but she'd heard plenty of tales from her kinfolk.

Secretly, she had always wished that a measure of her father's magic might have been passed down to her. But it seemed to have died along with him, and she had not been born with any sign of inheritance herself.

Each of Rodhlan's four outlying clans—Énna, Tarlach, Mór, and Beran—were meant to have inherited ancestral magic. But according to legend, the Rí's corrupt bloodline had stolen those powers from the people for centuries. Magic had once been commonplace among clanspeople, but over time, its wielders had dwindled to almost nothing. These days, most people—particularly city-dwellers—no longer believed in magic at all.

Among the clans, the few people who did inherit power wielded it in secret. It couldn't be suppressed, as power was designed to be expended. Those who manifested magic grew ill if they didn't discharge it from time to time, at the very least. Oda wasn't sure about clans Mór or Tarlach, but she'd heard that Clan Énna possessed few magic-wielders these days.

Clan Beran's power was concentrated among its healers and was quietly passed down from one generation to another.

She was surprised that the Crown hadn't tried to intervene in the clans' daily lives and had instead given the outliers a wide berth for many years. The late Rí Corlan had been known for his hands-off approach to the clans until his untimely death. Still, it appeared that his son was determined to follow in his footsteps.

Rodhlan was a small continent, and Iathium was its large, beating heart. The city held enough power over the land and its clans that there was little hope of any one clan ever overpowering it. As long as the city kept to itself and left the clans to their ways, everyone could go on as they had for so long: separately, quietly, and immersed in their respective traditions.

When Oda reached Ljós's door, she let herself in. But a torch was already lit inside the dim room, and from the threshold, she could barely make out the golden glow of healing magic. Abruptly, the magic flickered out.

"Who is it?"

Thorne's voice cut through the silence, and Oda froze. Her

mouth went dry before she gathered herself enough to say, "Oda."

A beat of silence. Then, "Oh."

She stiffened, memories of their sparring earlier flooding her mind. His words... "I'll come back when you're done here —"

"No. Come in and close the door behind you."

His baritone voice was tinged with anger. She hesitated for a moment, but there was no harm in doing as he asked one last time. By tonight, she would be gone, and he would no longer be giving her orders.

Oda stepped into the chamber and latched the door behind her. On her way across the room, she left the glass bottles on Ljós's worktable. Then, she turned toward the pit of amber stones in the center of the room. Today, they sat dark and untouched, a sight that made her swallow hard.

Ljós often used those stones for divination, particularly when he was unsure of what remedies to use for a particular ailment or injury. Oda had seen him illuminate them with power countless times. Their luminous resonance filled the chamber when they were lit, a healing force all on their own.

Oda could barely make out Thorne's silhouette on the other side of the stones. She could see that his torch was barely burning, now that the sunlight had been shut out. Hesitantly, she conjured a golden orb of magic in her palms and cast it into the stones to light the room further.

The magic drew Thorne's attention, and he turned to glance at her.

"Come here," he said.

To Oda's relief, his tone was already more subdued. Beneath the anger, she thought she heard a hint of dejection. She was torn between feelings of satisfaction and guilt at the realization. As much as he'd deserved the pummeling she'd given him, she almost felt remorseful for embarrassing the general.

Almost.

Oda obeyed, moving around the stone pit and sitting across from Thorne on the floor. He flicked his gaze upward for a moment to acknowledge her, then went back to conjuring magic. Summoning a small orb, he pressed it to his left wrist, letting the power absorb into his skin.

"You're hurt?" she asked tentatively. And *there* was the guilt, in full force.

"Small annoyances, no thanks to you." He sighed, his brows knitting in concentration. "I was able to clear all the others, but this wrist—"

"May I?" She scooted closer to him, moving onto her knees and reaching out with an upturned palm.

Thorne narrowed his eyes at her. "Do you intend on breaking it?"

Oda shrugged, biting her lower lip to keep from grinning. "I could."

"Then break it well." He extended his arm, and she gripped his wrist, scanning the tattooed runes along his inner forearm. "I trust you."

She snorted. "Bold of you to trust *sjivoc*." With her free hand, she skimmed the surface of his skin, noting changes in temperature, warmth, and the flow of energy.

Her hurt must have been obvious, because Thorne grew very still. He observed her as she worked, using her magic to make small adjustments to the bones and ligaments in his hand and wrist until they returned to equilibrium. She could tell by the subtle yet uninhibited flow of power in his body. It was a strangely intimate thing to be attuned to.

"*You* are wounded," he finally said. The accusation in his voice was unmistakable.

"No thanks to you," she echoed, placing her free palm over

his. She conjured golden magic and drove it into his warm skin, watching it illuminate his entire arm before dissipating. "I suppose you'll be demoting me now. Driving me out of the ranks."

"That's ridiculous." Thorne shuddered almost imperceptibly. "What are you doing here?"

She sidestepped the question. "It's a good thing I *am* here, or you might have begun the trials with an injured wrist since you didn't bother to ask anyone for help."

"You brought vials into my father's chamber. Did you come for supplies?"

She shifted uncomfortably. "Oh, I—Mum forgot her dandelion root and fennel. I thought Cynda and I might take them to her."

Thorne raised a brow. "So you changed your mind about staying, and you want to join Elda?"

"Um." Oda pressed her lips together as her cheeks grew hot. "Yes."

His gaze was searching. "Because she can get dandelion root and fennel anywhere. You don't have to take them to her."

She swallowed. "Yes."

He watched her pour more magic into his wrist. "It was unkind of me to goad you about what you call her. And to suggest your father's clan is disrespectful."

Oda pressed her thumbs along the insides of his wrist, feeling his bones move more fully into place. "I accept your apology."

"And to call you *sjivoc*," he added abruptly, almost in a mutter. "I shouldn't have said it."

"Oh." She was glad the room was dim; she hadn't anticipated the sudden pricking in her eyes. There was no way she would ever let this man see her cry over one of his insults. He'd dealt them before, but none had ever cut so deep. "I accept that, too."

"Is that why you want to go?" he asked, his voice taking on a gentle tone she had never heard from him before. It was gone almost as quickly as it had emerged. "If there's another boat, I will take you, if that's really what you want to do."

"I had not considered it before," Oda answered reluctantly.

"Until the arena."

She clenched and unclenched her jaw. "Right."

He pulled his arm from her grasp, rotating his hand carefully, then curling and uncurling his fingers. "But you were unsettled before we began," he said.

"Damn your healer's senses—so were you," she said, laughing in spite of herself. "Can I not have my own private feelings?"

"Can I not sulk alone in the dark?" he countered with a small smile. "Tell me what started all this."

"Only if you tell me why you joined the trials."

CHAPTER 5

THORNE

The trials. Oda's words sounded so accusatory. So bitter.

Thorne rocked back slightly to assess her. "You say that like it's personally offensive to you. Is there a problem with me leading the clan?"

"Leading through cruelty? Yes," Oda said, her gaze piercing. Her voice dropped to a whisper. "It's no better than the way Artur will conduct these trials, or the binding rite at the end."

She pressed her lips together and averted her eyes, as though she'd said too much.

Thorne sat up straighter, puzzled. "Why is that tradition a problem?" he asked.

"It's cruel!" she hissed. "Separating seven families for five years—not to mention ripping the heir's wife away right after the wedding night."

Thorne shrugged. "That's simply how it's done."

Oda gave him a deep frown. He wasn't sure why, but that look made him feel incredibly uneasy. Her first response to learning about his bid for the throne had grated at him, too. "'*Simply* how it's done?'"

"Hush." Thorne raised a hand, then flicked his fingers to cast the silencing spell Ljós had taught him years before. His ears popped, and he swallowed hard to release the pressure. "You know these corridors hear everything. Now, you can continue."

She rolled her eyes, then opened her mouth to pop her ears, too. In the two years since Oda had joined the Beravakt, Thorne had come to trust her as both a confidante and a leader among his warriors. It was the reason why they now found it so easy to spar with words, just as they did with blades.

Conveniently, his father knew an ancient spell that shrouded private conversations from outsiders, and Thorne used it liberally.

"Are you not worried about the repercussions of taking a wife, only to have her stolen from you immediately after?" Oda demanded, raising her voice now that it was safe to do so. "And what about her? You're accepting of *her* abandonment, too?"

"The privilege of Beran's throne demands great sacrifice. Five years is a small price to pay for a lifetime of serving the clan."

The words flowed out by rote, and he scarcely checked their meaning as he said them. He had always said them. He had always believed them. That's just how things were.

"Five years of secrecy. Separation." Oda nodded slowly. "And that's nothing to you."

Thorne turned his palms upward, as if to ask, *what else do you want me to say?* He wasn't prepared to admit that he hadn't truly thought this through. On the surface, the facts were what they were. It wasn't practical to think any further into the feelings behind them.

She narrowed her eyes. "Thorne."

He tilted his head, assessing her. "You want me to be worried about the physical separation. After consummating the marriage. Is that it?"

"*Consummating.*" Oda groaned and rubbed a hand over her face. "Coming from you, that word sounds like bedding a porcupine."

Thorne grunted a laugh. He couldn't help himself. "Artur chooses the wife. If I win the trials, I'll do my duty. That will be that."

"*Duty.* Berav, help me." She shook her head, though her eyes lit with mischief.

The corner of Thorne's mouth twitched in amusement as together, they quipped, "A most unworthy request."

Invoking Clan Beran's ancient deity had become a shared joke between them. Berav had been either silent or dead for centuries; no one was sure. Few of the elders still acknowledged him, and the clan's young knew nothing of his legends. Thorne's father had raised his son to pray dutifully to Berav, though his prayers had never been answered.

Oda wrinkled her nose. "Maybe you *are* the right man for the job. If you can ignite that spark and then immediately put it out *for five years*, then I commend you, and you deserve whatever you reap from your noble sacrifice."

He frowned. "You don't think I'm capable."

Now it was Oda's turn to laugh. "What man is? Make the treasure forbidden, and it's all he'll be able to think about, day and night. But maybe that's the point—to overcome an obsession with what you can't have."

"You think I'm like most men," he replied, "but I can control my impulses."

Thorne had no interest in the betrothal part of this role; to him, it was mere obligation, an essential part of the greater whole. He would do whatever he was asked to do if it meant fulfilling Artur's requirements to gain Clan Beran's Anointing.

Although he had never shared his feelings with anyone before, Thorne found that he took no interest in the young clanswomen who vied for his attention. He was only concerned with nurturing the few close friendships he had. Now that his father had returned to Iathium, he only had his childhood friend, Jund—Artur's nephew and the keeper of the fortress's hanging gardens—and Oda.

Oda had been by his side for long enough now that he wanted to be near her often. She was one of the few people in the fortress who was unafraid to challenge him—and to meet him as an equal. As embarrassing as his defeat had been earlier today, she had bested him because they were so evenly matched.

"Mmm," Oda hummed, raising a brow. "You come and talk to me about that when they've taken the treasure away."

"Why are you worried about it?" Thorne asked with a scoff. "It doesn't affect you."

Oda and her older sister were half Énna. Artur would want a Beran descendant whose bloodline had demonstrated loyalty over centuries; that was certain.

"I didn't think it would," Oda answered slowly. She chewed the inside of her cheek before continuing, "Mum was quite worried about it before she left, though."

He nodded in understanding. "So you were vexed with me, and Elda's worries made it worse."

"I thought that perhaps Cynda and I should move on. You have to remember, this will affect seven of our peers. Seven families we know and work alongside. It's going to be painful for the clan, not to mention the feuds that will arise among competitors' families when they're defeated or dead."

"I have a contingency plan for the feuding," Thorne replied evenly. "The Beravakt can keep that in check."

"I'm glad we have your confidence," Oda said with a wry grin. But the smile didn't reach her eyes.

Thorne rotated his left wrist and was surprised to still feel a twinge of lingering pain. He extended his arm toward Oda again, allowing her to seek out the source of the hurt. "What else is bothering you?" he asked.

Her touch was so gentle, such a contrast to her fierceness in combat. He fought the urge to close his eyes as she skimmed her fingertips along his skin again.

She was silent for a long moment before she answered him.

"Mum said our father had a deal with Artur to keep us out of consideration," Oda said softly. "I don't know the details, and she may not, either. But Papa was concerned enough that he made it part of their bargain."

Thorne knew that Uden Énna, later known as Uden Beran, had been close to Artur and had helped make the Fortress what it was now. He had also heard rumblings of the man's involvement in fortifying Clan Beran's defenses, though he wasn't privy to details. If he won the trials, however, he might be able to learn more.

Still, Thorne knew better than to share the notion with Oda. The two didn't need to hatch any schemes on the eve of the trials. There would be plenty of time to gather information later.

"If you still want to go to Elda, I'll take you," he said instead. It was the only offer he could fulfill.

"That's tempting," Oda hedged, "but it sounds like you'll need someone around to knock some sense into your thick head after you win. Like you said, it won't affect me."

Relief flooded Thorne's chest, but he held himself steady.

"If your father and Artur had a covenant, then they had a covenant," he replied. "And I know Artur well; he'll select a longstanding clanswoman for this role. If I win, we'll do our duty, and there will be nothing for you to worry about."

But as soon as the words left his mouth, his father's voice rang through his head.

"We had a covenant."

Yes, they had. Thorne had once promised Ljós that he wouldn't compete in the trials. But circumstances had changed, and he'd made the decision to break that promise.

What if Artur did the same?

~

"You were not yourself in the arena today."

Jund Beran approached the long dining table in the Arthmael's Hall. He set down a steaming bowl of stew, followed by a flagon of ale, as he took his seat. The stew was made from root vegetables Jund had helped to grow and harvest in the hanging gardens.

"Oh?" Thorne asked flatly. "Then who was I?"

His friend grinned, the flickering torches casting a shadow across his features. Jund neatly rolled up the long sleeves of his crimson tunic; he had always taken care not to soil his clothing at mealtimes. He picked up his spoon and stirred the stew. "Not the mighty general, that's certain."

Thorne curled his lip at Jund's candor before tearing a tender piece of pheasant meat from the bone and taking a bite. It was warm and flavorful, a welcome meal at the end of what had proven to be an incredibly long day. He'd been looking forward to enjoying the dining hall's comforting warmth, familiar bustle, and the mingling scents of fresh bread, smoked meats, and sweet mead. He was *not* in the mood to endure more of Jund's goading tonight. His friend's presence had been exhausting of late. Thorne wasn't sure when Jund had begun to repel him so, but the feeling had grown stronger over the past few months.

"How would you know?" Thorne replied. The response sounded more like a statement than a question. "You weren't there."

"People talk." Jund studied Thorne closely, clearly looking

for an opening. He had tied his wavy brown hair at his nape, which had served to accentuate his soft features. "That doesn't bode well for a competitor in the trials."

Jund appeared more like a warrior than a gardener, and Thorne had often ribbed him about his avoidance of joining the Beravakt.

"*I'd prefer to feed the clan rather than fight my brothers and sisters,*" Jund had always declared. "*You let me feed your warriors, and together we'll keep their minds and bodies sharp.*"

A wave of uneasiness swept over him. Instinctively, his gaze flicked to the high table, where Artur presided over the meal. The overlord's eyes were fixed on Thorne.

Training his expression into neutrality, Thorne looked back to Jund and replied, "Best to take what you hear with a little doubt." He shrugged, feigning nonchalance as he took another bite.

"No one speaks ill of you," Jund continued, scooping a spoonful of stew from his own bowl. "But there is... concern."

Concern. Thorne tried not to furrow his brow.

His friend's words were as carefully chosen as ever, so Thorne would need to be cautious in his response.

Jund might not be a member of the Beravakt, but he knew how to spar with words. His intellect was frighteningly quick, and he was always several steps ahead of the people around him. Had he been raised in Iathium, he would have made a skilled courtier or politician, gathering morsels of gossip and using them to his advantage. Gardening in the courtyard seemed to provide similar benefits, since he always knew what was happening in the fortress.

It was clear Jund was aware of what had happened with Oda in the arena. Usually, he reserved this gloating expression for debates he'd already won. Thorne heaved a long-suffering sigh.

"Why should anyone be concerned that one of my own

warriors bested me?" he asked, taking a hunk of potato from his plate. "The teacher has done his job when his students surpass him."

Jund's eyes lit with an emotion Thorne couldn't quite pinpoint, and he set his jaw. Thorne had always harbored a particular hatred for social maneuvering, and Jund knew it. Why should responding directly raise the man's ire?

"Not when his students have become his competitors." Jund took another bite, studying Thorne closely. "What will happen when you're bested during the trials?"

"That won't happen," Thorne said decisively, taking another bite of meat.

"If a woman can take you down, there isn't much hope." The corner of Jund's mouth twitched. "I would have never believed Tyr had a chance until today. Now, I question my judgment."

Jund's words were loud enough to draw the attention of the Beravakt nearest to them. Their conversations lulled abruptly. Several of them set down their flagons and spoons to glare at Jund.

Rynd, one of the younger Beravakt, adjusted the leather cuffs he wore around his wrists, clenching and unclenching his jaw as he regarded Jund. "Insult the general again, and you'll answer to all of us."

The other warriors rumbled in agreement. At the end of each day, they were in various stages of dress; most still wore their leather tunics and wool breeches, while some were further dressed down. All of them were armed to some degree, though none brought their full cache of weaponry to meals.

Still, those who still wore throwing axes and blades made sure to remind Jund of that fact. Rynd's fingertips drifted to one of the small axes at his side.

Thorne held up a hand to stay them. "Sit down, Rynd."

Tyr, the man in question, threw his head back and let out a

loud laugh, then drained his flagon of ale. He slammed it down on the table and shouted, "One more for the victor!" His words were slurred with drink.

Jund sneered, turning to shout over his shoulder, "That was not a compliment, Tyr."

Thorne's stomach suddenly felt sour. He frowned, taking a sip of water from a ceramic cup and swishing it in his mouth before swallowing. For a long moment, he stared Jund down, letting the silence drag.

Jund held his gaze without flinching, the hint of a smirk playing across his lips.

Finally, Thorne lowered his cup and said, "Do not goad me in front of the Beravakt, Jund."

Something in Jund's gaze softened, and he broke into the familiar grin Thorne had known since childhood. "An overlord requires a sense of humor. I should know; my uncle Artur has none."

Thorne's expression remained stony. "Humor isn't a requirement. Respect is."

Jund raised his brows in surprise. "Come now—"

"You are my oldest friend," Thorne interrupted, trying to ignore the nervous tension knotting in his stomach, "but I require your respect, especially in the presence of my warriors."

It wasn't the first time Thorne had needed to remind Jund of this all-important rule. Perhaps it was best that he did so today, before the trials began.

"Respect." Jund inclined his head and placed a hand over his heart. "No doubt, you'll make a fine miniature of my uncle."

A flush washed over Thorne, but he held steady in his seat. Held his tongue. Pinned Jund with a hard stare, knowing full well that Artur would be watching the exchange closely.

Leaning nearer, Jund added, "Now, let me offer you some truth: Don't let her distract you again. It was noticed."

Thorne shook his head, rising from where he sat. "You need greater responsibility to occupy your mind."

He didn't wait for Jund's reply as he crossed the hall, shoving the massive carved doors open and disappearing into the dark corridor that led up to his chamber.

CHAPTER 6

ODA

FIVE DAYS LATER

"Are you sleeping?" Cynda whispered in the dark.

"No," Oda replied.

The sisters had long since climbed into bed, and Oda was restless. She'd been trying to lie as still and quiet as possible so as not to wake Cynda. But it seemed her sister was just as unsettled as she was.

After Oda's discussion with Thorne, the sisters had agreed to remain at Fortress Halgeir. Thorne's reassurance had echoed Oda's own assumptions about the betrothal rite, so she had tried to let her uneasiness about the tradition lie.

After all, this was likely the only time her generation would see this event.

If she had children, though, *they* would have to worry about it. It seemed unlikely, but things could change.

Still, one thought continued to echo through her mind over and over. She had not been born among this clan, and she was no longer certain she wanted to die within it—or for it, for that matter.

For a day or two, she had managed to shove all thoughts of the rite from her mind. Instead, she had busied herself with preparations and training for the trials. As she'd hoped, Thorne had selected her to train with him and his fellow competitors. Oda was already certain he'd best them all; the coming challenges were mere spectacle and formality, and he was more than capable.

The memory of Thorne's insults still stung, and as the days passed, she'd found it more and more difficult to shake the hurt.

More than that, though, she was increasingly bothered by his declarations about the final trial. What made him so confident that he could withstand being deprived of his new wife for the five years of their marriage? Why did it grate on Oda for him to dismiss marriage as mere duty?

It shouldn't matter, and it didn't. As he'd said, she wouldn't be affected.

She willed that to be true.

Her sister's voice cut through her swirling thoughts. "I heard something strange in the courtyard today."

The words were low and cautious, so Oda propped on an elbow and moved nearer to the edge of her bed so she could better hear. "What was it?"

"I'm sure you've heard already, but in case you haven't," Cynda hedged, "there's talk of Artur taking a bride from Iathium. They'll wed after the trials."

The words descended on Oda like a slab of stone.

She scoffed, "Nonsense." But her heart began to pound, even as she protested.

"She's not even from Clan Beran," her sister continued, the words tumbling out faster than Oda could keep up. "She's from Clan Mór, *and* she has children who refuse to come here with her. One of them works for the Crown. Artur has agreed to pay their debts and house the pampered brats in Iathium."

Oda recoiled in disbelief. For years, she and her family had struggled and sacrificed to gain acceptance in Fortress Halgeir

—all because of Artur's rules. And now, Beran's demanding overlord deigned to break his own rules by putting an outsider with questionable family loyalties on the throne beside him. How would the clan be able to trust him as their leader after this?

"*Why* would he do that?" Oda hissed. "Those are *our* tithes. They're not his to spend at will—"

Her sister quickly beckoned her to stop speaking. "*Shhhh.*"

The two fell silent for a moment, listening carefully for any sign of noise outside their chamber door. The quiet was deafening.

When Cynda was satisfied no one was listening, she continued in a voice so low Oda could scarcely hear it. "Jund says this is a sign of things to come. He thinks Beran will gradually become friendlier to the city—it's just a matter of time until Artur hands our fortress over to the Rí as an outpost for his sentries and fills his pockets with our tithes."

"Surely not," Oda countered, already shaking her head in disbelief. "It's difficult enough to get in and out of here, and too far from the coast."

"Not from the eastern coast. Rumor has it that Macha plans to use her son's power to reestablish a foothold in the east. Clan Tarlach couldn't withstand a bid for its territory; they'd give up their settlement in an instant."

A small remnant of Clan Tarlach's once-vast settlement remained at Va'hesk, a sprawling encampment of tents and pastureland near Rodhlan's eastern coast. The continent had never experienced an invasion from the east as it had from its western coast, but that didn't mean the territory should go unprotected. Even Oda could see the logic in that.

Oda wrinkled her nose. "There's still Beran's Gorge to contend with. Sentries won't bother rowing upstream; too much work. It's why we've been insulated for so long."

"Well, I think Jund's argument has merit."

Cynda lay silent, letting the moment stretch.

Uneasiness crept into Oda's belly. She wasn't sure what was brewing between Jund and Cynda. Still, the thought of it gave her a full-body chill.

Of course, the idea of fleeing Clan Beran with Cynda had been frightening. The uncertainty of leaving with no plan for the future had been uncomfortable. But whatever *this* was felt like it scraped against the edge of treason.

Her instincts were confirmed when Cynda added, "He's going to challenge the overlord during the trials."

"*What?*" Oda's pulse thundered in her ears.

"Calm yourself, Oda," her sister demanded. Her next words tumbled out in a rush. "Jund says the inheritance shouldn't be determined by the overlord's choice. That is, if the overlord is weak."

Every one of Oda's senses went on high alert, and she sat up in bed. "Cynda—"

"I agree with him," her sister replied, sitting up to face her in the dark room. Determination glinted in her dark eyes, and she set her jaw. "As the overlord's nephew, Jund is the rightful heir if we consider bloodline."

Bloodline had never been a consideration in Clan Beran. It had always, *always* been about strength and selflessness. Cynda knew this, and so did Jund—and anyone else who was a big enough fool to consider treason.

"He'll get himself killed," Oda snapped, "and if you go along with him, so will you."

Her thoughts swirled. Jund and Thorne had been friends since childhood. If Thorne could hear this now, he would be enraged. There was no way the two could remain allied if Jund intended to challenge Artur for the throne. As a member of the Beravakt, she would have to report this to Thorne, and she had no control over how he or Artur might choose to respond.

Cynda's voice wavered a bit. "Maybe I can convince him to stand down."

Oda bristled. "And how will you—"

"He's in love with me."

We should have fled. Oda struggled to steady her breathing. *We had a chance to leave; we should have taken it.*

As if reading her thoughts, Cynda said, "Even if you had decided to leave the fortress, I would have stayed behind. Jund is prepared to fight for me if I'm chosen as the heir's betrothed. And that's not going to happen, anyway."

"Jund won't be fighting for anyone if he challenges Artur," Oda said through gritted teeth. "He'll be dead, and likely you with him."

"Then he *won't* go through with it. I'll speak to him."

Oda's nostrils flared. "You will *not*. Do you have any idea what sort of danger he has put us in? Not just you and me, but our entire family!"

"Do *you* understand the risk Artur takes, bringing in a *sjivoc* to rule beside him?"

The skin on the back of Oda's neck prickled. Even if this Mór woman wasn't the best match for Artur, she would be coming to assimilate into Clan Beran's culture. She would face just as many challenges as, if not more than, Oda and her sister had. Even though Artur would be relaxing his own decrees, the people would not easily accept these changes. That fact alone began to cool Oda's ire.

"I do agree there's risk in change," Oda said carefully, "but there's more risk in treason. I won't take part in these discussions, and I suggest you stop, too. Jund is in over his head, and he's going to drown you with him."

"What about our tithes? Are you no longer angry?" Cynda challenged.

"It's natural to react, but I'm sure Artur has his reasons. I shouldn't have spoken out of turn."

She couldn't see much detail in the dark, but she could make out Cynda's swift movement and hear the rustle of her furs being discarded. A moment later, Cynda's feet hit the cold stone floor of their bedroom.

"What are you doing?" Oda hissed.

"Going to find Jund," said Cynda, her tone harsh. "It's not long 'till dawn now. You won't see reason, and I refuse to argue with you."

Oda was too stunned to reply, and a moment later, Cynda had disappeared into the dark corridor, letting their chamber door shut with a bang.

CHAPTER 7

THORNE

Two more days.

Thorne drew in a deep breath of cool morning air as he wrapped the flexible strip of leather around his wrist. Slowly, he wound it up and around his palm, covering his knuckles before retracing his path and tying off the end. He flexed his fingers, testing the leather's resistance before starting on the opposite hand.

Two days left to train. Two days until the reckoning began.

From the beginning, Thorne had not worried about his ability to win the trials. Instead, he'd begun to wonder whether his father had been right. Had he joined only to satisfy his mother's memory?

Yes and no, he thought. *What I told sjeiva was true; the city's influence here is too great. We must not yield our homeland to Eremon. His warmongering mother will be the end of all the clans and their ways, just like Nami wanted.*

Nami was the ruler who had first stolen the clans' magic and slaughtered so many of its wielders two thousand years prior. Who had outlawed their languages in favor of Athi. Who, along with his bloodline, had amassed and hoarded unthinkable amounts of power for themselves at the people's expense.

Thorne shuddered, thinking of how his father had so dutifully chosen to act as Eremon's healer. Fleetingly, he wondered whether all that massacre and theft might finally be catching up to the Rí's bloodline.

One can only hope.

He had often questioned the stories he'd heard about Iathium's rulers. It didn't seem possible that they could simply store and pass down magic in their bodies in such a way.

After all, magic-wielders must discharge their power or risk death. It was one of the few known rules for people who possessed these abilities.

The bright early-morning sun warmed Thorne's face and exposed arms as he looked down over the courtyard. He stood by the stone railing nearest his chamber door, watching his fellow clanspeople moving about below. Jund and Cynda were already at their posts in the hanging garden.

Something about Cynda's posture seemed unusually tense. Her eyes darted about the wide-open space as she stepped nearer to Jund, who stood as still as stone, listening intently to her every word with a frown tugging at the corners of his mouth.

Thorne found himself bracing on the railing, straining as though he might be able to hear their words from up here. Oda's sister was so unlike her, instead willowier and more soft-spoken.

Like every woman raised at Fortress Halgeir, Cynda knew her way around a blade, but she was no warrior. She seemed more like a woman who aspired to raising children and keeping a home, whereas her sister relentlessly pursued one challenge after another.

He couldn't imagine Oda settling down for a quiet life. There was a wild, simmering fury beneath her collected exterior that he had always found fascinating. It was one of the many reasons why he'd been drawn to her, and why he had come to trust her as a leader among his warriors.

When she entered a room, her presence drew everyone's attention. That sort of spirit couldn't be taught; it was innate.

Movement from below brought Thorne's focus back to Jund and Cynda, the latter of whom put several paces between herself and Jund. The dark-haired young man, on the other hand, now peered up at Thorne. But rather than calling out a greeting, as he might have done before, Jund scowled and turned back to his work.

Thorne's brow creased with concern. Cynda, looking rattled, rushed out of view and deeper into the garden.

Strange.

With every moment, Thorne's mood darkened. He buckled his belt and adjusted the broadsword at his side, then started down the wide corridor, moving along the shadowy stone walls as he descended the spiraling fortress. By the time he reached the ground level, his scowl was deeper than Jund's.

Thorne crossed the courtyard in the direction of the gardens. But when he arrived, neither Cynda nor Jund were anywhere to be found. It was so early that most of the other gardeners had not yet come to tend.

It was rather curious that they'd been out here this time of morning.

Footsteps sounded on the path behind him, and Thorne turned to see Oda approaching. She looked deceptively calm, save for the deep distress in her eyes.

Oda had always been strong, but her full range of emotions was always visible in her eyes if one paid close enough attention.

He wondered whether she was aware of how much she revealed.

"You need fresh poultice for your sister's wound," Thorne

said without missing a beat. He jerked his chin in the direction of his father's chambers and began to walk.

Oda gave him a terse nod. "It's mending well, but yes. Thank you."

She fell into step beside him, saying nothing more. Absently, he wrapped his fingers around the hilt of his sword, white-knuckling it as they walked. It was torture to keep his mouth shut, even in the short distance between the courtyard and his father's chambers.

When they reached their destination, he locked them in and cast Ljós's silencing spell. "What's wrong?"

Oda plopped onto the floor beside the pit of stones and rested her head in her hands as Thorne began lighting his father's torches. "I don't want to tell you. But I fear if I don't, it'll make things worse," she sighed.

Thorne returned a lit torch to its sconce on the wall. "It's better to—"

"Why did you enter the trials?" Oda demanded, looking up at him. "You never answered me before."

His throat tightened. "I—"

"The *truth*, Thorne," she cut in, exasperated. "I just... I never imagined you as overlord, no offense."

"I felt it was right," he said carefully, edging nearer to her.

She raised a brow. "Because?"

"You're worried about speaking to me, yet you demand to know things I feel just as guarded in answering."

Recognition lit her eyes. "Ah. Then you feel the same way as Jund does."

"About?" he pressed, tilting his head.

"Artur's new bride. It all makes sense now; why you called me *sjivoc*, why you've been so agitated." She huffed and shook her head. "I knew something didn't seem quite right."

Oh. Thorne sighed. "And how does Jund feel?"

Oda's voice dropped to a whisper. "He feels Artur has no right to bring that woman here, and Cynda appears to agree."

His body tensed with apprehension, and his throat tightened.

"They need to be cautious. I saw them speaking outside. They'll draw the wrong kind of attention."

"And what about you?" Oda asked, lifting her chin. "If you agree with Jund, what sort of attention will you draw?"

"I will stay focused on winning the trials," he answered, pressing a palm to his heart. "Division is no good for Beran. When I'm overlord, I'll restore the clan to its old ways."

"Ah, the long game." Oda drew her knees up to her chest and wrapped her arms around them. "Honorable, to be sure. At least you're not blathering on about challenging the overlord."

Thorne went still, his body growing cold all over. "Challenging?"

Oda gaped at him, pressing her fingertips to her full lips. "I did *not* mean for that to burst out of me. I was trying for more tact."

It was suddenly difficult to hear her over the thundering of his heart. *Jund* would challenge Artur? To what end? How could Jund possibly lead the clan more effectively than his uncle when he knew nothing of protecting a fortress, much less conversing with basic tact?

It couldn't be. Perhaps Jund had only been speaking out of turn.

He shook his head to clear it. "He's a gardener, not a warrior."

"But he's Artur's nephew," Oda argued. "He thinks that gives him claim."

Thorne scoffed in disbelief. "Bloodlines mean nothing here, and he knows it."

"I told Cynda he'll get himself killed. She said she would

talk to him. I assume that's what was happening in the garden earlier, though I've no idea how he responded." She bit her lip.

"Unfavorably, I think," Thorne answered with a sigh. "I'll speak with him myself. If word reaches Artur, it will be Jund's head—the fool."

Thorne took a leatherbound box from his father's shelf with trembling hands and drew out the ingredients to make Cynda's poultice. He ransacked his memories, attempting to dredge up any clue that Jund had ever felt entitled to the overlord's throne. If Jund felt bold enough to issue a challenge, that meant he had support among the clan. But who would possibly go along with this?

With a mortar and pestle, Thorne crushed the herbs with more force than necessary, then mixed them with a bit of oil to make a paste. Then, he carefully transferred the poultice into a small glass jar, sealed the opening with a bit of cloth, and tied a thin leather cord around the container's neck to hold the cloth in place.

Thorne crossed the room and pressed the jar into Oda's hand. Whether she actually needed it didn't matter; she couldn't leave here empty-handed.

"I don't want this to escalate," Oda said, averting her gaze as she accepted the jar. "I doubt you do, either."

"You would be right," Thorne answered tersely. He moved toward the door but paused when Oda rose to follow. "I'll leave before you," he said, holding up a hand to stay her. "Give me ten minutes, then follow. Head for the arena. Not the gardens, and not your rooms."

She nodded, worry shining in her eyes. "Understood."

CHAPTER 8
ODA

Oda tried to keep her expression emotionless as Thorne studied her from his father's doorway. His eyes glinted in the torchlight, the alarm in them unmistakable.

She had never seen him so rattled—not even when she had bested him in the arena a few days ago.

He grasped the door's handle but hesitated.

"I don't want to risk exposing you, so I won't go to him immediately," he said slowly. "If Jund is stupid enough to say this to your sister, others may have heard it, too. I'll have Rynd gather information."

Without thinking, she reached out to grasp Thorne's forearm. "But the trials—"

"Begin in two days." A frown tugged at the corners of Thorne's mouth. "I'll need to speak to Jund before the sun sets."

Her eyes widened. "Today?"

Thorne nodded. "Today."

Oda drew a breath and exhaled shakily, dropping her hand. "What should I do until then?"

"Your usual," he answered. "Nothing out of the ordinary if you can help it."

"Fine." She gave him a terse nod. "I'll do as you ask and make for the arena. Maybe I'll even give you the upper hand today."

His gaze warmed, and he offered her a pinched grin. "I'm counting on it." For a moment, his expression shifted; his brow creased as he tilted his head. "Is there anything else I need to know about this business with Jund?"

If Thorne was going to de-escalate this situation, then there was no need to mention his friend's feelings for Cynda. Jund had merely said he was in love; that did *not* mean Cynda returned his feelings.

Regardless, Oda could manage talking sense into her sister. If Thorne could handle Jund, then Oda could handle Cynda. Discretion would be their most powerful ally in this situation, even from one another.

"N-no," she stammered, mentally kicking herself for the blunder. "There's nothing more."

Thorne raised a brow but nodded. "Meet me back here after evening meal, and I'll tell you what I learn."

The tightening in Oda's throat eased. "Until then, I'll see you in the arena."

"Keep your wits about you," he replied with a smirk. "You're going to need them today."

CHAPTER 9
THORNE

The afternoon sun was high when Thorne abandoned the arena in search of Jund. His body ached from exertion, his muscles taut. Oda, Rynd, and his competitors had worked him to near exhaustion in the sparring ring, but the physical release had been welcome.

All day, he had turned the conversation with Oda over and over in his mind.

Why would Jund risk outright treason by speaking so freely around the fortress? Rynd had been able to validate Oda's claims, and Thorne was now armed with everything he needed to confront Jund.

He just wished things could be different.

The most difficult part of all of this was that, on a fundamental level, Thorne agreed with Jund.

By bringing an outsider to rule beside him, Artur was going against everything he'd ever stood for. Keeping Clan Beran strong should have remained his priority. Opening their fortress to more of the outside world would leave them too vulnerable to influence from the city and the other clans.

Still, confronting and doing battle with Artur wasn't the

answer. If Jund challenged Artur outright, he would get himself killed at worst, and exiled from the clan at best.

As angry as Thorne felt about his foolishness, losing one of his only friends was also a reality he didn't want to explore.

There had to be a way to fix this before it went too far.

"I know that expression." Thorne whirled from his position at the garden's edge to find himself face-to-face with the very man worrying him, who offered him a wry smile. "Word travels quickly."

"We should speak alone." Thorne's gaze darted all around them for a safe place to converse without prying clansmen listening in. He couldn't use his father's spell unless they found an enclosed space first. "This is foolishness."

"It is necessary," Jund countered, taking a step closer and lowering his voice. "Don't tell me you agree with what's happening."

"I will say nothing here," Thorne replied stiffly, clenching his jaw.

There was a knowing glint in Jund's dark eyes. "And by saying nothing, you say everything." He lifted his chin and added, "I know you, Thorne. You didn't enter the trials out of loyalty to *him*. We want the same things; we're not enemies."

"Endangering the clan is something an *enemy* would do," Thorne countered.

Jund raised a brow. "You see? The last thing either of us wants is to endanger the fortress."

Thorne blinked in surprise. He hadn't meant for Jund to take his statement as an agreement.

Even though he secretly agreed.

If Thorne was determined to lead Clan Beran, he would need to appear as loyal to Artur as possible. He just hadn't anticipated standing against a friend in the process.

A cold chill swept through him as a realization settled. If Jund's treason went any further, *Thorne* might be forced to execute him. As leader of the Beravakt, it was almost guaranteed. The very notion made bile rise in his throat.

He shook his head, though his heart began to pound. "You will force my hand if you continue down this path."

"The *sjivoc* has no proven loyalty to this place," Jund hissed. "Only to Iathium. If you would just—"

"Enough."

"My brother—"

"Don't." The courtyard was still eerily silent.

Heat spread from Thorne's belly up his torso, into his throat, and down his arms as he clenched his fists.

He took a deep breath, letting it out slowly before saying, "I'm asking you to trust me and stand down. Whatever you're trying to prove, it won't be worth the price."

Jund barked a hollow, disbelieving laugh. "You would rather play at valor than hear what I have to say?"

"I would rather we all stay alive." Thorne hated this tension that was growing more taut, more palpable, between the two of them with every passing moment. And he hated the gnawing fear he felt at the possibility of being overheard and implicated. "For the sake of our future, you should reconsider your position."

For a long moment, Jund glared, his upper lip curling in disgust. He spat on the ground, then raised his gaze back to Thorne. "Not *my* future," he said before turning and striding away.

Once Jund had cleared the area, Thorne stalked toward the shadowed corridor, where he had ordered Rynd to wait for him.

A worried expression marred the younger warrior's youthful face. Thorne was sure it was identical to his own.

"You heard all?" Thorne asked in a low voice.

Rynd nodded. "I did."

"Keep watch." Thorne's words were almost inaudible now. "We'll do what we can to silence him before this goes further."

THORNE DIDN'T WAIT until after the evening meal to find Oda. He sought her out in the arena half an hour later, where she was overseeing the trainees' drills. Even from the top of the stairs, he had no trouble picking out her position.

She stood in a wide stance, her arms crossed, surveying pairs of warriors as they took turns sparring on the far end of the arena floor.

They fought with wooden swords and axes, taking slow, deliberate steps through their drills as she looked on. Her back was to him, so he couldn't see her expression, but he imagined a satisfied smile on her face as he moved down the wide staircase in the direction of the floor.

The eighteen trainees Oda oversaw ranged from about ten to twelve years old—the youngest group in rotation. At age fifteen, they would be eligible to enter the Beravakt ranks if they so desired, and if their skills fit Thorne's rigorous requirements. So far, all of them looked like they would be up to the task when their times came.

When Thorne reached the arena floor and crossed in Oda's direction, the pair of trainees who had been practicing lowered their wooden swords.

The young boys watched him approach with mirrored awe in their expressions.

"Back in position," Oda barked before she turned her attention to Thorne.

We need to speak. Now.

He saw a flicker of understanding in her eyes. Oda seemed to have a particular knack for knowing what he was going to say before he uttered a word. Like so many times before, he hoped that she had managed to get the message today.

"At ease," she said, turning back to the young fighters. "Never stop fighting to ogle a superior. Beravakt warriors are expected to keep their eyes, hearts, minds, and bodies always engaged. Don't let anyone or anything distract you from that purpose."

"Unless you've been called to attention," Thorne added, looking to Oda in a silent plea for permission.

Oda nodded once. *Granted.* "In formation," she commanded.

The young men and women fell into their ranks, assembling before Thorne and Oda with their training weapons at rest. Thorne scanned their faces. Each held his gaze unflinchingly, still and silent as they awaited orders.

"Dismissed," Thorne said.

Once the young trainees disbanded, he turned to Oda. She was kneeling on the arena floor, securing her blades in their scabbards. Her calm demeanor set him at ease. Knowing about Jund's treason was enough to put Thorne on edge, but she seemed to be bearing the information well.

When she rose, weapons in hand, she raised her chin and said, "I've mapped out modified drills for the trainees to continue during the trials. Could I have your ear?"

Relief filled his chest at her command of the exchange. He still hadn't been sure what to say, only that he needed to speak with her *now*.

Thorne nodded. "War room. Follow me."

CHAPTER 10

ODA

Thorne pushed the heavy door to the empty war room shut and cast the silencing spell the moment they were safely inside.

This room was located near the arena floor, down a cavernous stone corridor. Artur, Thorne, and the Beravakt often used it to plan defensive drills. Less often, the senior Beravakt used it to chart out training plans for the young warriors in secret.

This sprawling chamber was also the location where Artur's collection of secret scrolls and maps were hidden. Where ink, quill, and paper were safe from the prying eyes of the clan. Clan Beran's own limited records of history, mythology, magic, language, and battle strategies were kept here, as well.

Unlike Iathium, Clan Beran seemed to care about passing on its true knowledge and pure culture to its people.

Oda had always reasoned that this was why Artur had always been so adamant about keeping outsiders away. He appeared to be concerned about making sure his people knew their history.

On the other hand, this clan made sure its people knew little of the city or the surrounding clans.

Oda popped her ears as Thorne's spell took hold. She would never get used to that.

"My father once spent many nights locked away in here with Artur," she said, looking around the dim room as Thorne lit the torches. "What I wouldn't give to know the secrets they exchanged."

"They're likely among the scrolls," Thorne replied, his brow furrowing as he sat at the wide stone table in the center of the space. "Once the trials are over, maybe I'll get a chance to look."

Oda pursed her lips. *If you survive the trials,* she wanted to say.

She shook herself mentally. Thorne *would* survive them. And he would win. There was no doubt about that.

Rather, she doubted Thorne's ability to hold true to that suggestion. Once he began his real apprenticeship to Artur, he would not enjoy the freedom to share everything he learned. It was a nice idea, though.

Striding over to the table, she lowered herself onto the bench across from Thorne. "So tell me what you know. I assume it's something useful since you changed your own plan and rattled me back there."

Thorne smirked. "You were not rattled."

"So you believe." Oda rested her arms on the cool stone of the table. Thorne's appearance in the arena, albeit ahead of schedule, had unnerved her. She hoped the trainees hadn't noticed the change in her demeanor at his approach. "Stop stalling and answer me."

"I confronted Jund," Thorne began, lowering his voice despite the spell's efficacy. "He wasn't himself."

She frowned. "You mean you couldn't sway him."

Thorne closed his eyes for a moment. "He has chosen his side. Now we must try to stop him from acting."

"Treasonous words are more dangerous than treasonous actions," Oda mused. "Words spread and take root amongst the people before anyone lifts a finger."

"And then you have an army of dissidents," Thorne said.

Oda nodded, her throat going dry. She wished she hadn't spoken against Artur at all, even to her sister. Dissent put outsiders in danger most at Fortress Halgeir. Even when a born member of the clan spoke out, distrust against the few outsiders who resided here was always amplified afterward.

"Do you think many Berans feel how he does, now that word about the city woman is getting out?" Oda asked, thrumming her fingers on the stone.

"I'm certain they do. But this isn't the first time we've calmed a storm within the fortress. I'm hoping we can get ahead of it."

That was news to Oda. She sat up straighter, tilting her head as she scrutinized him.

"What do you mean, not the first time? I assumed it was rare."

This clan had always been so outspoken about loyalty. She couldn't imagine Thorne controlling dissent on a regular basis, much less preventing it from reaching Artur's ears.

"Not rare," Thorne hedged, "but also not frequent."

"Yet this is the first I've heard of it." She narrowed her eyes as the full truth of the realization settled in. "Because I'm a *sjivoc*. I see."

Without fully knowing why, she rose from her seat on the stone bench. Thorne sat up straight, instantly on alert, his eyes fixed on her face as she took a few steps back.

Two expressions she rarely saw crossed his features in quick succession: concern, and then conflict.

"Oda."

She froze at the sound of her name. Thorne rarely used it to address her outside of training, so hearing it in this context somehow felt different, especially with the plea she detected as he added, "That isn't why."

Her shoulders sagged as she exhaled, planting her feet where she stood. "Don't lie."

Thorne blinked, then ran a hand through his hair. At some point this afternoon, he had unbound it.

"I am not," he countered.

Oda refrained from rolling her eyes. She had noticed that he sometimes wore his hair loose when he was worried or under stress. He also had a habit of running his hands through it when he was being dishonest.

When she took another step back, he held up his palm. "Wait."

"One chance," she said, making a show of glancing over her shoulder at the door. "You get one chance to be completely honest."

"Fine," he said, casting his gaze to the ceiling as though Berav himself would materialize to grant him mercy.

Undeserved, Oda thought. She smirked. "I'm listening."

"It's a risk to speak to outsiders of dissent. I won't unless it's necessary," Thorne said. "But"—his eyes filled with an intensity that made her face feel suddenly warm— "that's true of my fellow clanspeople here, too. And of the overlord."

Oda's brow furrowed. "You don't tell Artur of dissent?"

"Only when necessary. You know what the consequences are. We all do. So when my spies or I hear tales of unrest, we end it quietly. No one here wants to see their loved ones face that fate."

Clan Beran's laws against traitors had been unspeakably brutal over the centuries. Penalties for openly disagreeing with the overlord's word were harsh enough, including public flogging and various methods of torture. At worst, plotting or attempting treason earned dissenters a slow, painful death at the hands of the Beravakt.

"Who helps you silence these incidents?" Oda asked quietly.

"Rynd," Thorne answered, looking a bit reluctant as he did so. "Mjit. And Ljun." He shifted uncomfortably. "Would you sit back down now?"

"Would you trust me to help you if I hadn't brought you this information?" Oda asked, refusing to budge.

He looked taken aback by this. "These matters must be kept small."

"That's not what I asked." She took a deep breath to steady herself. Anger was building in her chest, but she wanted to remain in control of it. "I asked if you trust me."

Thorne's lips parted as though he was unsure what to say. Then, to Oda's surprise, he rose and crossed the room in her direction.

She peered up at his towering form, waiting for him to admit that no, he didn't trust her. Next, he would suggest they leave and return to their duties.

They would avoid one another for the foreseeable future, and Oda would have been handed a harsh reminder that she didn't belong at Fortress Halgeir, and she never really would.

She nearly yelped when Thorne reached out and placed a large hand on her shoulder.

"Yes, I trust you," he answered seriously, bending a bit to level with her. "You've been my only real friend besides my father and Jund. And now they're both gone."

Oda swallowed hard, her heart suddenly racing. He was close enough that she caught his familiar, earthy scent—sage and cedar, mingled with salty sweat. "You think me a friend?" she whispered.

Not only a friend, his *only real friend* now. It was difficult to wrap her mind around the concept.

A smile tugged at the corner of Thorne's mouth. "Are you going to make me say it again?"

Oda blinked, shaking her head and taking a step back. "No, no, I—it just took me by surprise. I thought I'd only begun to win your trust."

"You have had it," he replied, withdrawing from her and crossing his arms. "Why else would I let you train the young ones? Why would I speak with you about the rite?"

She huffed a laugh, mirroring his movements and folding her own arms across her chest. "You're right. I've been foolish."

"Stop telling yourself you don't belong here. No one else feels that way about you" he said gently, as though reading her thoughts.

There couldn't have been a more infuriating time for tears to prick her eyes. For her chin to tremble. For one tear to trickle down her cheek faster than she could swipe it away.

And then for Thorne to notice and to close the distance between them again.

He looked down at her, worry in his eyes as more tears began to fall. "What can I do?"

"Keep your mouth shut about this," Oda said, voice wavering slightly. She gestured towards her crumpled face and runny nose.

"Fine," he said in mock resignation.

She wasn't sure what propelled her forward in the next moment.

Perhaps it was the sheer emotion of having no one at home to comfort her right now. But the next thing Oda knew, she had thrown her arms around Thorne's brawny torso and was embracing him, her cheek mashed against his chest as she quietly wept.

He froze, as though he wasn't sure what to do with his arms. But then he wrapped them around her gingerly and let her lean into him.

Thorne's embrace was more comfortable and familiar than Oda had been prepared for. Now that it was happening, she realized she'd always assumed that any sort of physical contact with him would feel awkward or strange.

But why would it? They had fought and grappled in the arena countless times.

Deep trust was required between trainees who came to blows on a daily basis yet still emerged as friends in the aftermath.

Friends. Thorne wasn't just her general; he was her *friend.* And he thought of her in the same way.

After a few minutes, Thorne patted her back. "We've been here for a long time. You'll need a moment to calm your face."

Oda laughed against his chest. "Calm my face?" She pulled away long enough to conjure a small golden orb, then swept it across her puffy eyes, feeling them clear right away. She looked up at him, crinkling her nose. "There. It's done."

He laughed softly, surveying her. "So... I mustn't tell anyone you cried."

Oda shook her head. "Or about this." She squeezed him for emphasis.

"Duly noted." Thorne stepped back as she released him. "You don't cry, nor do you seek comfort. You are Oda, the merciless warrior queen."

"That sounds like the stuff of legend," she said with a smile. "And don't worry; I won't be advertising your free hugs. We need the people to fear you. What happens in the war room is the stuff of blood and gore."

He snorted. "Right."

They laughed together, the sound relaxing the tightness in Oda's throat.

"I'll let you know if you can help me with silencing Jund," Thorne said, steering them back to the topic at hand. "This is the first time in years that I've doubted myself in this way. Jund is much angrier than I expected, and I worry that his words have spread too far already."

"Let me deal with my sister," Oda answered, her lips curling down with worry. "I can start there. She wouldn't hear me out last night, but I want to try again."

"I'll look for Jund at evening meal," Thorne said. "Come to me if anything happens."

"Likewise," she said with a nod.

Together, they moved toward the door. Oda touched the handle but paused, looking back over her shoulder at Thorne.

"Thank you for that," she said softly. "I mean it."

"I accept." He smiled, then jerked his chin toward the empty room behind them. "Blood and gore, yes?"

Oda nodded with a grin. "Blood and gore."

THORNE

That evening, Thorne stood before the doors to the Arthmael's Hall. He didn't often linger near the elaborate carvings, but tonight, the images had caught his attention and held him there. They told the story of Berav, Clan Beran's infamous silent god.

For a long moment, Thorne studied the depictions of battle, magic, and lore, so lifelike they seemed to move in the flickering torch light.

If only Berav was willing to answer prayers—to intervene in this impossible conflict that was unfolding.

With a sigh, Thorne shook his head and pushed the heavy doors open. When he beheld the stone-silent room, he stopped in his tracks. He scanned the hall, starting with the tables nearest him as he swept his awareness throughout the sprawling space.

Warriors sat at table as always, but there were none of the usual sounds of dining and conversation. The mood was low. Much more than it should have been, with the trials beginning in just a few days.

He'd scarcely noticed the thrumming excitement that had

buzzed through the fortress over the past week, especially since this business with Jund had begun.

Now, though, he keenly missed its absence.

Finally, he let go of the doors and warily strode into the hall. Rynd met him halfway to his usual table, pressing a steaming bowl of stew into his hands. Alarm flashed in his dark eyes.

Thorne felt a disconcerting sweep of energy over his body as all the attention in the room turned to them.

"Dine with me," Rynd said.

Thorne nodded, accepted the bowl, and followed Rynd to his table. They sat across from each other. One of the serving maidens brought them cups of ale, and Rynd took a long swig, then drew the back of his hand across his mouth.

"What has happened?" Thorne asked.

Rynd leaned near to answer, his eyes flicking to either side of them before his lips parted.

"The overlord has brought his intended to Fortress Halgeir," Rynd answered in a low voice. "She arrived today and will dine with us tonight."

Thorne felt as though he might be sick. "You're certain?"

Rynd inclined his head. "I saw her after we spoke. She was accompanied by sentries from the Dome. No armor, of course."

"Why before the trials?" Thorne numbly pushed his spoon around in the stew. "I don't understand this."

"No one does," Rynd replied.

But then Thorne's entire body tensed, and he found himself clenching his teeth. "Is Jund aware?"

"Mjit and Ljun are dealing with him. I'll fill his seat tonight; otherwise, his absence will be that much more obvious." Rynd drained his cup in a few long gulps, then made a fist and pounded the table. "More ale. We're going to need it."

He raised his hand to summon a serving maiden, but Thorne said, "Wait."

Rynd raised a brow, stroking his beard. "Sir."

"Who is she? The Mór woman."

"Her name is Iva," Rynd said. "She's nine and thirty but looks younger than her years. Long, dark hair—and pretty."

Artur's first wife, Gild, had been a warrior in every sense of the word, as well as a devoted follower of Berav. Her faith had been strong, despite the ancient god's silence over so many centuries.

The people had mourned her untimely death as a confirmation of Berav's own demise, something they had long speculated behind closed doors.

He directed his thoughts back to Iva and wondered again at Artur's choice. The overlord had never expressed a desire for children and had none of his own. It was strange that he would now choose to provide for stepchildren, whether they came to live with him or not.

Thorne shook himself, bringing his awareness back into the hall.

"Should we greet her?" Rynd asked, tapping the bottom of his cup on the table's worn wooden surface. "No one knows what is to be done."

The Beravakt had received no word that visitors would be arriving. Thorne imagined that if Artur had wanted to make a spectacle of Iva's arrival, he would have already done so. Usual protocol dictated that official visitors to the fortress would be met with ceremony.

"The overlord is not one for guessing," Thorne ventured, taking a spoonful of stew and blowing on it. "We continue as usual."

Rynd shrugged, waving a hand for his cup to be refilled. "Perhaps he wishes for her to see life as it is here. Decide if this is what she wants."

"You could say that if the trials weren't beginning so soon."

"Maybe she'll be gone before the start."

Thorne took a long drink of warm ale. The journey to Fortress Halgeir from Iathium wasn't a terribly long one, but it was harrowing by way of the gorge. Artur and the overlords before him had ensured that access to the fortress was as difficult as possible.

"Unlikely," he finally said.

He glanced to the high table where Artur took his meals. The overlord's usual seat was still empty, and there had not been a second chair brought in. Where did he expect Iva to dine?

He thought about the sentries Rynd had mentioned. Perhaps, if Iva had guards, Artur had not wanted to bring them into the hall. That made sense.

Still, the uneasy feeling in Thorne's gut grew more insistent. It was possible Artur had no intention of bringing her to table at all. His gaze swept the hall, and he began to take note of the missing faces.

There were at least seven empty seats on the floor, seven warriors absent from their normal routines.

Oda and her sister weren't here, either.

At the realization, his heart began to thump erratically. This was one of the worst times and places to panic; he couldn't use magic to calm himself before the warriors. He must clear his head.

Thorne forced himself to slow his thoughts, to remember that this wasn't unusual.

Oda and Cynda normally took meals in their chamber or in the courtyard with the healers. It was a habit from childhood they'd never broken.

Again, he looked to the empty high table. As the word *trap* slowly drifted through his mind, the doors to the hall slammed open behind him.

Thorne rose and turned to see Jund stride inside, fully armed, an axe and sword sheathed across his back. His dark eyes were blazing with fury, and his jaw was clenched as he stopped just inside the hall. A small contingent of men from the clan—six, at a glance—entered behind him, brandishing weapons of their own.

To Thorne's relief, none of the men were from among the Beravakt ranks.

Thorne rose, adrenaline pumping through his veins. A quick scan revealed that Jund and his men had clean skin and garments. Some of them wore leathers, although none were fully protected. There was no trace of blood or dirt, so it was clear they had not yet seen combat.

Still, they were armed more heavily than the warriors tonight. Even without the Beravakt's elite skill, they could do serious damage to the people in the hall.

Anger surged through his body at the thought. Thorne was lightly armed with two small axes and a large dagger strapped to his outer thigh. None of the warriors ever brought large blades or axes to table, though they were all armed similarly.

Thorne wasted no time drawing his axes, though he held them at his sides, just as he held his friend's stony gaze. Behind him, he could hear his warriors and the others in the hall rise.

In Artur's absence, all eyes were on him. On Jund.

Jund met Thorne's gaze, then flicked his own toward the high table. His brow furrowed when he found it empty, but the expression was gone as quickly as it had come.

"Where is my uncle?" Jund demanded. "And the *sjivoc*—we had hoped to greet her."

Advancing a step, Thorne answered, "You have an unusual manner of greeting."

His heart thudded, and he silently prayed to Berav's memory that no one else in the hall could sense his trepidation. His grief. The shock and heartbreak of staring into the murderous eyes of a man who had once been his friend.

Dead eyes. Like the fallen god he pleaded with in vain.

He tightened his grip on his axes. "Leave the hall, Jund."

Jund scoffed. "And leave the high table empty?"

Ah. Now, it made sense.

The pieces fit together swiftly in Thorne's mind. Artur had indeed set a trap.

By leaving the high table empty and letting it be known that Iva was present in the fortress, he would draw the rebels out. He had left his seat vulnerable for whomever was foolish enough to attempt taking it.

"You'll force my hand," Thorne warned in a low voice.

Jund smirked. "That has already happened. Now, my friend, step aside so I can take what is mine." He raised a hand, surveying the room as he addressed the others present. "Let us restore Clan Beran to glory."

"This is not glory," retorted Thorne. "People will die."

His pulse thundered in his ears. He could feel the other warriors in the hall rising behind him, taking their positions with what few weapons they had. Jund and his small band *could* do damage before they were inevitably defeated. How much, Thorne couldn't predict. But he would do what he could to secure the fortress.

Jund offered him a small shrug and drew his axe. "That is their choice."

The men who stood behind him assumed fighting stances, too—just like they had growing up in the training arena. As though Thorne and the Beravakt would waste time posturing in kind.

No pretense, Thorne thought grimly as he swiftly launched one of his axes across the space between himself and Jund. *Only action.*

The blade lodged firmly in the sinew between Jund's neck and shoulder, sinking to the collarbone and rendering his right arm useless. Blood soaked Jund's tunic as he howled, his axe clattering to the stone floor. He crashed to his knees, and the men behind him retreated a few steps, looking at one another as though suddenly unsure of why they'd come.

Rynd and the other Beravakt warriors took their cues then, charging the stunned men as they let loose battle cries.

Amidst the clamor, Jund ground his teeth, groaning loudly in shock and pain. Thorne felt as though he might be sick as he watched his friend try to reach for the axe's handle. Jund's hand trembled so violently he could not grip it without screaming in agony.

Swallowing his nausea, Thorne kicked the larger weapon out of reach, then wrenched his own axe from Jund's shoulder. The man cried out as the blade tore away, bright blood pouring from the open wound.

Fury and betrayal were etched in Jund's expression as he looked up to meet Thorne's eyes. Then, Jund snarled, grasping for his sword with his functioning hand.

Lunging forward, Thorne trapped Jund's arm, locking his left shoulder so he couldn't reach the broadsword's hilt. He applied enough pressure so that Jund's entire body went rigid, resisting further pain. With a quick shift of his weight, Thorne used what leverage he had to propel Jund toward the floor.

He maintained enough control so that Jund's face didn't strike the stone, but rather stopped just short of it. In one smooth motion, he swiped Jund's broadsword, then let him drop to the floor. Thorne hefted the sword, then positioned the tip of its blade against Jund's back.

"Beravakt!" Thorne forced the order from his lips, fighting against the tightness in his throat. The disbelief that had not fully settled within him that this was truly happening; his own friend had betrayed both him and their overlord. "Subdue the traitors."

"No!" Jund tried to push himself up with his good arm but collapsed again when he felt the sword's point against his spine. "I share Artur's *blood*!" he shouted.

"And I'll spill all of it right here," Thorne growled, applying more pressure to the blade.

Jund turned his head just enough to leer up at Thorne, a mocking smile crossing his lips despite his pain. "Go ahead. Or are you afraid?"

"Quiet!" Thorne pressed the sole of his boot against Jund's left upper arm, pinning it down.

"What will you do when you're ruling alone?" Jund snarled. "When the little bear can't hide behind the overlord's might?"

Little bear. It was what Jund's mother had once called Thorne when they were children many years ago. The words drove into his heart like a jagged blade.

Thorne knew he shouldn't listen. He should drive the sword down; it would be a mercy for the traitor's death that awaited Jund at Artur's hands. Instead, he found himself frozen where he stood.

"What will you do when the people finally see you panic?" Jund laughed bitterly, his cheek pressed against the stone floor. His dark gaze drifted away from Thorne and to some distant focal point as he added, "That boulder you carry is heavy, my friend. You will never be able to hide it from them."

A warm grip on Thorne's wrist tore him from Jund's words, and he turned his attention to Oda, who now stood at his side. Her tunic was blood-soaked, and she gripped her bloodied axe, her eyes wide.

"It's over," she said in a low voice. He didn't miss the slight tremor as she spoke.

Thorne made a quick sweep of her body, noting wounds on her bare shoulder and lower lip that would need attention. Her posture, the tension in her stance, betrayed her discomfort, and he guessed she might also have hidden injuries to attend to.

"Put them in cells." Thorne raised his voice for the warriors. "Then return here when it's done. Rynd, Mjit—take Jund."

"Stay where you are."

Artur's voice boomed from the hall's entryway. The hulking warrior-king strode into the vast room as though this moment had been perfectly orchestrated.

Thorne turned to him, offering a reverent nod. For the first time since subduing Jund, he took in the scene around him.

Two of the men who had stormed the hall—middle-aged traders with whom Thorne was only vaguely familiar—lay dead in their own blood. The others had been subdued and disarmed. His Beravakt were in a state of disarray, but none besides Oda appeared to bear significant injuries.

She hadn't been here when the conflict began. When had she arrived to fight?

Two unfamiliar men and two women wearing black tunics and trousers fell in behind Artur, armed with swords at their hips.

One of the men led a wary-looking woman whose long, brown curls had been plaited into Clan Beran's style and woven with beads and bits of bone. She wore a plain gown of cream linen, a decorative leather belt slung low around her waist.

There was a slight pallor to her skin that betrayed her origin: Iathium.

This must be Iva.

Her discomfort was apparent, but she held herself with poise. Rather than letting her attention linger on the prisoners or the dead rebels, she looked to Thorne and gave him a small nod.

"You passed your first test," Artur said, offering Iva his arm but keeping his eyes fixed on Thorne. "The trials have begun."

CHAPTER 12
ODA

Oda strained to keep her eyes on Artur, who was still standing in the doorway. Curiously, his form blurred, then returned to focus.

She blinked in a futile attempt to sharpen her vision, then tried to draw a breath. Sharp, burning pain lanced through her side beneath her ribs, and she stopped short, holding her breath until it passed. Again, she tried to breathe deeply. This time, her vision went white from the pain, and her knees suddenly felt weak.

Artur was still speaking, yet she had missed—how much *had* she missed? She took a few short, shallow breaths through her nose, forcing her attention back to him.

"I commend your loyalty, Thorne," he was saying. "And yours, my Beravakt. You also have the gratitude of my intended, who I'll wed once I choose my heir."

The overlord's normally booming voice drifted in and out of earshot, fading and returning in a puzzling way. She gave her head a subtle shake to clear it, but a wave of dizziness overtook her instead.

For a moment, she almost lost her footing. Taking a few

more short breaths, she attempted to right herself. Collapsing among the ranks wasn't an option, and certainly not in Artur's presence.

Steady, she thought. *Let him finish. He will go. Then, you can sit.*

Oda tried again to take a full breath. This time, the pain was more intense, and she had to press her lips together to stifle a groan. Taking on two fully-armed men wouldn't normally have resulted in injuries this extensive, but tonight, she had been thoroughly distracted.

That distraction had come with a high price: a few superficial wounds, and what felt like multiple shattered ribs, from her best guess.

One of Jund's rebels had bludgeoned her side with a heavy club, and she had not been prepared for the impact. He'd thrown his whole body weight into it, knocking the wind from her so fully that she had dropped her axe.

Oda had been unable to prevent a second rebel from catching her and pinning her arms behind her back while the first attacked. He had only managed to split her lip with a poorly-executed punch before two of the Beravakt had come to her aid.

On any other day, she would have been able to defeat him single-handedly.

She shouldn't have come to a fight in this emotional state. But because of Cynda's relationship with Jund, Oda could leave no room for anyone to doubt her loyalties. Especially Artur.

And especially since she had restrained and drugged her sister before coming here.

Maybe Oda had accidentally ingested some of the sedative herself. Was that why she felt so lightheaded? So weighed down by exhaustion?

"I will draw out the rest of the traitors," she heard Artur say over the sudden roaring in her ears. "And they will receive the deaths they deserve."

Her chest was *so* tight. Now, her lungs burned, and she needed to *breathe*. But when she tried once more, little bursts of white light mingled with shadow, and she could no longer see the warriors, the overlord, or his pretty, frightened *sjivoc* bride.

Oda felt her knees buckle and her body sway. Before she lost consciousness, she felt strong arms catch her. Lift her. Hold her close.

And then she let herself slip away.

CHAPTER 13

THORNE

Thorne gathered Oda in his arms and ran toward his father's quarters.

He'd caught her right before she hit the ground. Perhaps it was wrong of him to have trained his attention on anyone other than Artur in that moment. After all, the overlord was a jealous ruler and craved all eyes on him.

But Thorne hadn't cared. And any worthy ruler would understand a general's concern for one of his warriors.

Oda's head lolled against his chest as he moved. She was dead weight in his arms, her breathing shallow. The usually faint scent of her healing magic was strong; it smelled of the autumn apples that grew in the groves just outside the fortress.

He imagined it working within her already, sparking and shimmering as it sought out all the wounds Thorne had yet to assess.

It wasn't that Beran's healers could regenerate with no help. But the presence of this magic in their bodies primed them for healing. With help from other magic-wielders, their wounds were capable of stitching together more quickly and completely than those who had not inherited birthright magic.

Thorne slowed his gait as they reached the healer's chamber, and Oda groaned at the shift in movement. He shushed her, cradling her body. Now that she was in his arms, she seemed so much smaller. It wasn't in her nature to collapse, to be rendered completely helpless like this.

As a member of the Beravakt, Oda had sustained more than her share of injuries, just like the rest of them. But her mother and sister had always intervened. On the more serious occasions, his father had stepped in to assist.

Thorne had never assumed full responsibility for healing her himself. The thought rendered him short of breath as he crossed Ljós's threshold.

Carefully, Thorne lowered Oda's body onto one of the healer's cots and lit the lanterns. Returning to her side, he ignited golden healing magic between his palms and began a slow sweep along her energy field. The superficial wound on her shoulder wasn't deep, and he was able to repair it quickly. But the broken ribs he found, the punctured lung, those wouldn't be so easy for him to heal alone.

The unexpected scent of salt tickled his nose, and he tuned in to the magic that swirled within her. Golden power radiated stronger than moments before, but beneath that, there was a current of magic he'd never detected. He closed his eyes, seeking more information.

A hint of violet power caught his attention, its color flashing through his consciousness, but it was there and gone in a breath. Oda had once spoken about her desire to know whether she had inherited water magic from her father. It had never manifested as an ability, and it was no wonder; how could she possibly harness such a small, fleeting spark?

Oda groaned, and Thorne's eyes snapped open. He studied her as she struggled to rouse herself, wincing in pain as her lashes fluttered.

For a moment, she seemed to have trouble focusing, but when her green eyes locked on his, he grew very still.

Despite her injuries, there was a fierceness in her gaze that directly contradicted the pain she was in. She looked ready to rise from the cot, take up her weapons, and storm back into the hall for another round.

The expression on her face took Thorne aback. So much so that his magic abruptly dissipated.

With a hiss, Oda gripped her side and closed her eyes. "Bludgeon me again, won't you?"

"Berav's ear," Thorne said through gritted teeth. Heat flooded his face. "I'm sorry."

He summoned more magic between his palms and directed it toward her ribs and the punctured lung beneath. Oda's body appeared to relax, and after a moment, her expression softened again.

"There's something you should know," she whispered.

"Don't try to speak," Thorne countered.

"I must," Oda said, opening her eyes to glare at him. "Cynda is in our chamber. Sleeping."

He didn't like the implication beneath her tone. "Sleeping."

"On my orders."

"Why?" Thorne asked, as nonchalantly as he could. "Is she unwell?"

"No." Oda hissed as Thorne continued to sweep his power over her body. "But I slipped a dose of *sjepdraught* into her stew."

Thorne's brow furrowed. "My father's tonic."

"He perfected it, indeed," Oda said. "She was asleep within three breaths."

Not only was Cynda asleep; she wouldn't remember enough in the morning to blame Oda at all. The herbal draught his father had created left behind no trace, as well as none of the usual aftereffects of being drugged.

Clanspeople who struggled to sleep peacefully through the night could take a small dose with no ill effect in the morning.

"It must be used sparingly," Thorne said. "I don't know when he'll return from Iathium."

"Kept her away from the hall, though, didn't it?" Oda said. She looked as though she was trying to smile, but she grimaced instead.

Thorne's frown deepened. He didn't want to think of Jund and the rebels right now. "It did."

Oda tried to take a breath but winced again. "You know that just hovering your magic over me won't heal my ribs."

"I—" Thorne shook himself. "I was preparing."

She raised a brow. "You think you can't do it."

Thorne grunted, conjuring more power to sweep over her. "I've never been good at mending wounds. These may be too severe for me."

"Not if we're working together."

Thorne shook his head. "You can't. You're wounded."

"I have a theory," Oda argued. "We combine our power. Double the magic—faster healing."

If Thorne hadn't been afraid of hurting her again, he would have stepped back in protest. But a moment ago, when he'd broken his flow of magic, it had hurt her.

Healers worked in tandem often, but they always shared a patient. Thorne had never seen a case in which the healer was both patient and, well... healer.

"I know what you're thinking," she said, "but I can't afford a long recovery."

"I don't think you have a choice," Thorne retorted flatly. "Perhaps with a more skilled healer—"

"No, it needs to be *you*. If Artur knew the extent, he'd make me take leave."

Thorne scoffed. "And I won't?"

"*You* need me for the trials," Oda said, her voice bordering on a plea. "And Cynda needs me to keep her out of trouble."

"I *don't* need you in the arena injured. And you should stay out of your sister's trouble."

"Just *try*," she begged. "What's the harm?"

Thorne studied her expectant face for a long moment, then sighed heavily. "Fine. But if this doesn't work, I'm going to find a better healer. Maybe two."

"Fine," Oda agreed. "I think skin to skin will work best."

Thorne blinked. "Skin to skin?"

"Yes," she said, grasping his wrist and pulling one of his hands toward her face. "Like this."

Oda pressed Thorne's fingertips to her split lip, and he sighed as healing magic fled his body and poured into the wound.

Her mouth was soft to the touch, and he was surprised to feel disappointed when the injury healed almost instantly. He withdrew his hand, his fingers tingling from the exchange of magic and the feel of her skin.

"Gods, that's better," she said, running her tongue over her bottom lip. She grinned. "I think my experiment worked. Now, let's heal my side."

Thorne nodded, gathering more of that golden power into his open palm. He watched as Oda gingerly undid the buckles on her leather vest, opening it to expose the loose linen tunic she wore underneath. He reached for the corner of the vest and held it for her as she untucked the tunic from the waistband of her brown leggings. She pulled the fabric up to expose her bare skin, her full breasts hidden only by the strip of thick fabric she'd used to bind them.

"This is the worst of it," she said, pointing to her lower left ribs, "so start above and work your way down. Focus the power beneath the ribcage, of course, then summon it to the surface so it can mend everything along the way."

An inexplicable tremor wracked Thorne's body, and his magic wavered. "Beneath your binding?"

"Yes. I suppose you'll have to cut it." She gave him an apologetic grimace. "The thought of trying to unwrap is nightmarish."

The sudden sweat that broke out across Thorne's exposed skin must have been from nerves. Surely, that was all. He ran a hand over his face, then nodded, pressing his lips together.

"Thorne." Oda pressed her hand over his, and his attention snapped back to her. "It hurts to breathe. I need you to focus."

A nervous huff escaped from him as he shook himself back to the present. "I need a dagger."

"Here." Oda patted her thigh, where a small blade was sheathed.

Thorne reached for it and drew it from its sheath, then turned his attention back to the thick fabric binding around Oda's torso. He sat on the edge of her cot for better access.

Gingerly, he tugged the bottom of the wrapping at her side, lifting it away from her skin so he could work the blade beneath it. With painstaking precision, he cut the fabric to split it open.

Oda pinched the ends of the ragged fabric with her left hand, tugging it just enough to prevent it from slipping completely out of place. Muscles tensing, Thorne kept his eyes trained on the bruised, now-bare skin over her ribcage. Her breath caught, and she took several uneven, shallow inhales.

"Now, Thorne," she whispered. "Before it gets worse."

"It won't get worse," Thorne promised, pressing his palm to her exposed skin.

His ability to conjure healing magic stalled at the contact, but he willed it forward. Golden power flared beneath his hand, sinking into her skin to search for the deepest of her wounds. Thorne closed his eyes, following the magic's path.

After a moment, he felt Oda's hand cover his. Her magic

was warm, though weak. It moved first through Thorne's hand, then joined his healing power, amplifying the current that flowed beneath her skin to knit bone and sinew back together.

Thorne looked at her then, and she held his gaze, drawing a longer, deeper breath than she had moments before. She winced at the end but gave him a small nod as if to say, *it's working.*

Encouraged, Thorne poured more of his healing power into her body, relaxing into the odd familiarity of touching her like this. He found himself drawn to match Oda's breathing, allowing his awareness to settle fully on her rhythm.

With each passing moment, those breaths grew steadier and stronger.

In tandem, the flow of her magic grew stronger, too.

Healing had never felt like this before. Discharging the magic had never been particularly satisfying for Thorne; it was more like a chore to be maintained. But there was relief in using the power alongside Oda. A deep, soothing sensation that grew warmer and brighter the longer their magic mingled.

He could see a flare of gold reflected in her eyes as their powers expanded outward, then burst from beneath their palms.

Gold healing magic surrounded them in ribbons and swirls, dancing and winding around their bodies as Oda's ribs began to mend. Thorne glanced down in wonder to where their hands met. Shimmering, golden magic shone on her dark brown skin, amplifying the beauty he had always admired into an ethereal thing. Fleetingly, he imagined that this was how a goddess might look, shining with the brilliance of her own astounding power.

"I'm going to break the connection," she said, her voice clear and powerful now.

She took a breath and removed her hand from his. Immediately, the power that had been swirling around them a moment before dissipated. Thorne took a moment to scan for her wounds and found that none were left. With a surprised laugh, he let his own magic fade before withdrawing his hand.

His fingertips brushed her side as he moved away, and he thought he saw her shiver before she closed her eyes.

"You're cold," he said, intending to rise from where he sat beside her. "I'll get you a fur."

"Wait," she commanded, shaking her head. "Help me sit up."

Hesitantly, Thorne offered her his hand. Oda rose with ease, then took a deep breath. She grinned, eyes shining. "It worked. You did it!"

Thorne failed to suppress his own smile. "Ah, well, you helped a bit."

She clapped a hand around the back of his neck, startling him as she pulled him to meet her. They pressed their foreheads together, an old Beravakt greeting reserved for times of victory and narrow escape. Once again, in tandem, they shared a breath.

Thorne found himself returning the gesture, his hand drifting up to the back of her neck, beneath her hair. But for some reason, he couldn't bring himself to clasp Oda like a brother—a fellow warrior, even.

Instead, he felt the urge to be gentle. To keep his touch tender.

After all, she had just been gravely wounded. And despite her rapid healing, she still required rest and time to recover.

Thorne's fingertips moved of their own accord, grazing over her warm skin. He savored the feeling of goosebumps rising in response. Oda gasped, the small sound almost inaudible.

Her fingers relaxed on his neck for a moment. As he trailed his hand down to rest on her shoulder, he felt her grip the collar of his tunic, bunching the fabric.

"Shall I test my strength," she said quietly, "by throwing you across this chamber?"

Thorne grunted, drawing back. "Then we would have more healing practice to do."

Oda laughed, releasing him and shoving his chest with a palm. "It was effective enough. Maybe we should try."

Thorne wasn't sure what possessed him to do it, but he cupped her cheek. The moment that had just passed, whatever it had been, couldn't dissolve so quickly. He wouldn't let it.

She stilled at his touch.

"We should," he said gravely, brushing his thumb over her cheek before pulling away. "Your idea was a good one."

CHAPTER 14

ODA

Oda was short of breath again. This time, for an entirely different reason.

But there was no time to think about what had just occurred between her and Thorne.

The moment he released her, the door to Ljós's chamber burst open. Thorne stepped aside, turning to greet Artur, Rynd, Mjit, and Iva Mór.

Suddenly, Oda was keenly aware of her open vest and the breast bindings Thorne had cut away. She had been holding the fabric down until she sat up, when she'd let her tunic fall back down to cover her body.

Still, she was unaccustomed to any of Clan Beran's men seeing her at less than her best—especially the overlord.

"Stand between us, Thorne," Artur ordered. "She is not rightly cloaked."

Oda's cheeks heated. Thorne did as he was commanded, but not before reaching for one of the furs he'd offered her earlier. It was draped over a stool just paces away from him, and he handed the rich, thick blanket to her.

She nodded her thanks, accepting the fur. Their fingertips

brushed as he released it, and she shuddered at the contact. Thorne moved to block Artur's view of Oda as she hastily shrugged back into the sleeve of her vest and pulled the fur up to cover her filthy, bloodstained clothing.

At least everyone believed her to be cold and still rattled from her injury. In reality, she was an inferno. Those brief, quiet moments with Thorne had unlocked feelings she'd buried so deep, she wasn't sure what to call them. There was no time to figure them out, either—especially with the overlord in the room.

"You are required in the dungeon to deliver justice." Artur's voice filled the chamber, saturating the stone surrounding them. "Both of you."

"Lord," Thorne said, inclining his head slightly in assent. The movement was subtly tense, and Oda hoped Artur wouldn't notice the shift in Thorne's usual demeanor.

A small female voice chimed in, "Your pardon, overlord."

Oda peered around Thorne's shoulder to catch a glimpse of Iva, whose brown eyes had gone wide. Her voice carried the lilt characteristic of Clan Mór's mountain people, though it was slightly more refined. *That* was clear evidence of her city heritage.

Artur turned to Iva and peered at her, as a father assessing a daughter he had little patience with. "You wish to speak?" he said in Athi.

Iva gave him a demure nod, clasping her hands before her as though she suddenly regretted the decision to say anything at all. "Yes, Lord."

"You may," Artur replied, to Oda's surprise. And then he added, "But you understand there must be consequences. *Sjivoc* must never be seen advising the overlord, married or no."

Iva set her jaw but nodded. "As you wish." The words seem to catch in her throat before emerging. She looked to Oda, faltering imperceptibly before she began. "The young warrior —what is your name?"

"Oda, my lady," she said. Athi felt awkward and unfamiliar in her mouth; it had been so long since she had spoken it.

"Oda." Iva smiled warmly, though there was apprehension in her eyes. "You're wounded."

"Yes," Oda answered, a nervous chill skating over her skin.

Iva took a step closer, wrapping her arms around herself. "How extensive are your wounds? Have you the strength for the dungeon?"

"I'm strong enough," Oda said, "but I'll need fresh clothing."

"Your wounds," Artur pressed, watching Oda closely. "My lady asked after your wounds."

Oda tried her best not to recoil at the hint of offense in his voice. "Your pardon, my lord. I suffered bruised ribs, a split lip, and lacerations to my shoulder. All healed now, I assure you."

She would suffer no reprimand for being hurt; after all, she had helped to stop the traitors in their midst. But if she were to reveal the full extent of her internal injuries, she would be placed on leave. Although healing magic could repair severe wounds, extra rest was always required in the days and weeks that followed.

If Oda were relieved of her duties right now, even temporarily, she couldn't be of help to Thorne during the trials —or the other warriors, for that matter. Right now, being near him was of the utmost importance.

"You fainted in the presence of my Beravakt," he observed. "Perhaps you can explain that."

"Exertion, Lord," she said quickly, her heart beginning to pound. "I took a hard fall, and the wind was knocked from me."

"A rebel fell atop her afterward, Lord," Rynd chimed in. "One of the dead ones."

Iva paled. "That would be enough."

After a long, tense moment, Artur lifted his chin, his eyes flicking to Thorne. Oda tried not to sigh audibly with relief.

"Thorne, your healing skill has grown in your father's absence," Artur said. "It's just as well; he's worth ten of you underlings. You will all need to improve your magic to make up for our great loss."

"Yes, Lord," Thorne answered.

The deep rumble of his voice set something fluttering in Oda's chest, and she bit back a grin. Whenever Thorne spoke in Athi, his cadence was more measured and deliberative than it was in Brylla. He despised the city's language, so he had not bothered to refine it. But that was precisely why she enjoyed hearing him navigate it; there was something endearing about the way he so carefully formed the words.

Artur jerked his head toward the chamber door. "It is decided. Thorne, you will accompany us to the dungeon. Iva, go with Oda to retrieve her things. She will bring you to the dungeon afterward. I wish for all of you to bear witness to justice."

Oda's shoulders tensed, but she nodded. "Yes, Lord."

Thorne didn't look in her direction, but instead followed Artur and the other warriors from the chamber, latching the door behind them.

Iva visibly relaxed after their departure, huffing a nervous laugh and pressing her hands to her now-rosy cheeks. Oda wasn't sure what to make of this slight woman standing in the center of Ljós's chamber, shaking her head as though in disbelief.

When Iva looked up at Oda, a wide smile spread across her lips. "What have I gotten myself into?" she asked quietly.

"The same thing we're all in, I suppose," Oda answered with an apologetic grin. "I am also *sjivoc*, it pains me to say."

Iva's eyes lit. "Ah, hailing from where?"

"I'm half Énna. I live here with my mother and sister."

"It's no wonder you were under scrutiny," Iva breathed. "If you don't mind my asking: How bad was it, truly? Surely not *just* bruised ribs."

Oda wasn't sure why she trusted the older woman so easily, but she said, "Broken ribs and a wounded lung. Fortunately, they're mended now."

"But you should be cautious," Iva said, her expression turning grave. "You needn't give yourself away through overexertion, if you take my meaning."

With a grimace, Oda nodded. "Oh, I understand completely."

"If not for the trials, Artur might expend more energy in testing your word," Iva said.

Oda held the fur around herself and swung her legs to one side of the cot. Cautiously, she stood, feeling a brief rush to her head as she did so. She held steady for a moment, then took a deep breath.

"You're right about that," she said.

Her first few steps between the cot and the door felt wobbly, but with each one, she grew stronger. Her footing steadier. Together, Oda and Iva put out the torches around the chamber, then emerged into the dark stone corridor.

The moon had long risen, and there was a slight chill in the air.

"Is it not late in the evening for justice to be served?" Iva asked tentatively.

Her tone took on a slight, mocking depth that almost made Oda chuckle. No one poked fun at Artur in the open air this way; certainly not outsiders.

"Justice supersedes all, save for reverence," Oda answered quietly as she led Iva in the direction of her chamber. She pulled the fur tighter around her shoulders. "This is the most serious offense the clan has seen in my lifetime; perhaps longer. He'll deal with it swiftly, and then we'll go about our lives."

She hoped she sounded convincing, but she wasn't so sure. If Artur discovered that Cynda had been party to the rebellion in any way, the best Oda could hope for was banishment. But if being summoned to the dungeon to *witness justice* was any indication, Artur wouldn't deal with Cynda kindly.

Oda would be deemed guilty by association and likely driven out.

"Tell me about your life as a warrior," Iva said as they walked. "None of the men seem very talkative—your general, least of all."

"Oh, I..." Oda stammered, her mouth going dry. "Thorne. He doesn't have much to say, no."

Inwardly, she cursed herself for stumbling over her words.

Iva's attention on her seemed to grow weightier.

"That is, none of the warriors are overly talkative," she added hastily. It wasn't the best recovery, but maybe it was passable.

"Of course, it seems Thorne has little need for words." Iva clasped her hands behind her back, offering Oda a coy smirk. "The way he raced out of the hall with you in his arms said plenty."

"He's concerned with the warriors' wellbeing," Oda sputtered.

How had this conversation taken such a turn?

Iva stopped walking and turned to face Oda, forcing her to stop as well. She leaned forward conspiratorially. "Would he cradle any of his other warriors to his chest like a fragile treasure?" With a tilt of her head, she laughed softly. "No? I thought not."

Never had Oda felt so exposed by an outsider to the clan.

This woman wouldn't last a month at Artur's side. They weren't even married, and she was already volunteering for his *consequences* in order to speak her mind—whatever those entailed. Oda supposed they were about to find out.

She must have gaped at Iva for a moment too long, because the Mór woman grasped Oda's forearm and leaned near.

"I apologize, Oda. My own daughter is more interested in the city's histories than its young men, and besides, I won't be seeing her often from here on. I'm afraid I leapt at the opportunity to goad you like I might goad her. Forgive me."

Sadness flashed across her features for a moment.

Oda seized the chance to change the subject, trying to ignore Iva's comments about young men and Thorne's overly gentle cradling abilities. "Tell me about your daughter."

"Ah, Silira." Iva pursed her lips, then gave Oda a slow nod. "Let's walk. I'll tell you about her."

They turned their conversation to Iva's daughter, whom she affectionately referred to as Lira, as they walked the wide, spiraling stone pathway that led to Oda's chamber. Oda reveled in breathing the open air freely; before the injury, she had taken for granted how good it felt to fill her lungs. She directed Iva's attention toward the areas of significance in the fortress, like the gardens, the entrances to the interior corridors, and the downstairs pathway to the healer's chamber they'd just come from.

Along the way, Oda learned that Iva's daughter Lira was an archivist in Iathium's infamous Dome, where she helped to preserve the ancient historical records. She had elected to stay behind in the city, despite her mother's decision to come to Fortress Halgeir.

Oda refrained from asking why the Rí bothered to preserve writings that no one was capable of reading. Only the city's historians and a handful of its rulers and officials were legally allowed to read these days.

"Do you have any other children?" Oda asked, pausing outside her door.

"A son, Talfryn," Iva answered. "He wanted to stay with his sister. Fancies himself a sentry. He's thirteen years to Lira's sixteen."

Oda nodded. "Ah."

"I miss them already." Iva gave her a pinched smile. She pressed her lips together, looking down at the ground briefly before meeting Oda's eyes again. "But we do what we feel we must."

The loaded remark caught Oda off guard. She was flooded with the sudden urge to ask what exactly Iva meant by that. But this wasn't the time nor the place to pry.

"My sister is asleep inside," Oda whispered, reaching for the door's latch. "You won't wake her; she's a heavy sleeper. So if you wish to come in from the night air, you can follow me."

Oda almost winced at her own lie, instead training her expression into something she hoped was neutral. Iva nodded.

"I think I will," she said, glancing around the corridor. "This place is still so unfamiliar."

They slipped inside, and Oda made quick work of re-binding her breasts and changing her clothes. True to her word, Cynda was still fast asleep, drugged into oblivion. Oda was glad she wouldn't be awake to witness what was about to happen tonight.

She shivered. Would Jund be executed? Would her sister wake in the morning to learn that her lover was dead? Not to mention the slaughter he'd attempted on the clan.

Oda tried to shake off the dread that filled her, but it was no use. She'd never been close to Jund, but Thorne and Cynda had. Keeping Cynda out of trouble remained her top priority, but now that Jund had openly committed treason, she felt gravely aware of his looming fate.

CHAPTER 15

THORNE

One step into the dungeon obliterated every ounce of healing magic Thorne had used on himself on the way here. Panic filled his chest, and a sheen of sweat broke across his skin. When he emerged from the long, dark corridor into the gloomy audience chamber, the scene that awaited him nearly drove him back into the shadows.

Artur's prisoners knelt side by side on a low stage against the room's far wall, chained together with shackles around their necks. Their hands were bound behind their backs, and their wounds had not been tended. Blood seeped from the gashes and sullied the stone floor.

Jund was in the center, the only traitor whose eyes weren't cast downwards.

They locked eyes long enough for chilling, stony hatred to seep into Thorne's gut. But Thorne broke the contact swiftly, scanning the other prisoners instead.

He could not let emotion overtake him here.

A low, twisted laugh broke from Jund. Still, Thorne trained his focus anywhere but him.

He couldn't allow himself to become sentimental now. Jund

was a traitor; he had endangered the clan. His fellow rebels had wounded Oda and some of the other Beravakt in the Arthmael's Hall.

Perhaps Thorne could have forgiven Jund's errant tongue, but he would never forgive what had happened to Oda because of it. Or the fact that he'd involved her sister and risked implicating her entire family in his scheme.

One of the men slumped forward with a groan, and Thorne caught a glimpse of bloody whip lashes across his back. The dirty, torn, stained linen of his tunic stuck to each oozing gash. Thorne guessed that all the prisoners' backs were in a similar state, and he had to suppress the urge to heal them.

After all, an overlord wasn't a healer, nor could he ever be.

Thorne's father had raised him with an instinct to heal first. But if he was to silence his late mother's belittling for good, then Thorne would need to be strong.

For now, he must push those feelings aside.

Artur's booming voice filled the audience chamber as he emerged from the shadows on the opposite side of the room, Rynd and Mjit flanking him. "A pity you missed the start of the flogging, Thorne. But you're in time to finish it."

Thorne straightened, though nausea roiled in his gut. "Lord?" He thanked Berav's memory that the word came out strong. Anything more and he might have choked on it.

"Give my nephew a traitor's due," Artur sneered, jerking his chin in Mjit's direction.

The young warrior stepped forward, extending the handle of a thick, gruesome whip to Thorne.

The overlord hissed, "Let him see what comes of betraying his clan. His blood."

The whip's ends were tied off with bits of bone, rock, and broken pottery to deliver much more pain than a singular lash.

Thorne had heard stories of the lashings this weapon could deliver, but he'd never seen or used it himself. Judging by the blood smattered on Mjit and Rynd's tunics, he guessed they had been the ones to start the torture.

"We'll see how you compare to your warriors," Artur continued, fixing Thorne with his powerful, intimidating stare. "Despite their youth, I'm tempted to allow them to join the trials. As of now, Tyr is your only opponent."

Before Thorne could ask what had become of the other three, Artur filled him in.

"Mund fled the fortress at the first sign of the rebellion and will not be allowed to return. Nyft is dead."

"And Ani, my lord?" Thorne's palm had begun to sweat around the whip's handle.

"Ani recused himself in the aftermath of the hall," Artur answered. "Wise of him."

Thorne inclined his head. "Yes, my lord."

"Now." Artur began to pace the wide, dark audience chamber between Thorne and where the prisoners knelt. The oblong room was built with a platform-style stage against its far wall, with plenty of space for observers to watch torture and execution proceedings. Historically, some prominent punishments had been carried out in the arena, but the dungeon prevented large crowds from gathering. In most cases, a smaller audience guaranteed the overlord's control of the narrative. "We will await my future bride's arrival. It's only right for her to witness what is to come."

Thorne tried not to wince. What a terrible welcome for the sheltered Iva. He wondered whether she would even be capable of standing, once she entered and beheld the prisoners.

Jund's eyes followed the overlord's every move. The pure contempt in them caused Thorne to tense.

How had he never noticed this undercurrent between them before? Thorne had spent most of his life absorbed in his love for Clan Beran and its ways. He'd believed Jund felt the same, but how could he, after everything he'd done?

But maybe he still *did* love the clan. After all, it was Artur who had shown signs of altering tradition. That had been the fuel behind the failed rebellion.

Thorne and Jund had been equally enraged at hearing the news of Artur's outsider bride. But Thorne's solution had been to focus on becoming the heir and to right these wrongs in the future. Staging a coup like Jund had just attempted would have never worked.

And the proof was kneeling here before them, covered in blood and writhing in pain.

His heartbeat picked up pace in his chest, pounding in his ears. How could he lash Jund, knowing he had said similar things about Artur himself?

You can't do it. His mother's voice echoed in his head, and he nearly lost his grip on the whip. *You won't. You're not capable— too tender-hearted. Too like your father.*

Footsteps echoed from behind, jolting him from his thoughts. Thorne turned to see Tyr Beran enter the audience chamber.

"'Evening, m'lord," Tyr said in Athi. He turned to Thorne with a nod. "Thorne. Suppose loyalty, or the lack of it, always shows itself. What say you?"

Thorne didn't answer. He tightened his fingers around the whip's handle, tempted to use it against Tyr first. His grating swagger was more abrasive than Thorne remembered.

Tyr sniffed, turning away. "As friendly as ever."

The taller, red-haired man two years Thorne's senior was lanky, ruddy, and strong, with jagged scars that marred the left side of his otherwise handsome face. The tale behind them involved pirates of unknown origin in the Olyran Sea, but something about that story had never rung true for Thorne.

"Ah, Tyr, he has no reason to be friendly," Artur said with a rich laugh, moving toward the stage but keeping his back to the prisoners. "Thorne is your only competitor now."

A sly grin crept across Tyr's face. "And we all know how much he hates to lose."

"We will see," Thorne said, lip curling back over his teeth, "since you could not be bothered to prepare with the Beravakt."

"Why, when I'm not one of you?" Tyr scoffed. "I have my own ways of doing battle. You'll see."

Thorne refrained from rolling his eyes, something he'd grown used to seeing from Oda. He wasn't sure what it was about Tyr that brought out this childish urge to fight back, but staying in control of his responses was of utmost importance now.

Tyr was a roguish braggart who had spent his teenage years and the first half of his twenties accompanying his uncles on trading missions to Iathium and beyond. His stories of adventure outside Fortress Halgeir had always made him seem discontent at home.

But at the trials' announcement, he had taken a sudden interest in putting down roots as Clan Beran's next overlord. A falsity if Thorne had ever seen one. Or a desperate grab for power.

Like Oda's family, Tyr's had been at liberty to come and go, unlike most of Clan Beran's people. Despite Beran's self-isolation and Artur's pride, it had always depended partly on trade to survive. Perhaps Artur had seen Tyr's ability to navigate Rodhlan's many societies, and even Iteloria's, as a political advantage.

More and more, it was becoming clear that Artur was aiming to strengthen bonds beyond the fortress's walls. But that meant opening Clan Beran to outside influences more than ever before.

Echoing that thought, Iva and Oda entered the chamber together. Iva immediately moved to Artur's side, but Oda paused in the entryway, her gaze pinning Thorne where he stood.

He forced away the memory of their magical exchange in his father's chamber, focusing instead on her appearance. No— her wellbeing, he told himself.

She was dressed in fresh breeches and leathers that hugged her generous curves. Her skin was clean and unmarred, and she carried herself as though she had not been wounded at all. The only clues as to what had happened in the Arthmael's Hall were the subtle, tired circles beneath her eyes.

Thorne glanced at Tyr, who was also watching Oda carefully. There was a hunger in his leer that made Thorne's skin crawl.

"This begins yet another trial," Artur said, pulling Thorne's thoughts back to the prisoners. "I've tasked Thorne with completing the lashing. The traitors have been allowed a short respite, but it's time to have this done."

All the men except for Jund began to groan and droop.

After a moment, Thorne understood why. Artur had Mjit and Rynd force the chained men to their feet. They were led to face the far wall, and then Thorne caught a glimpse of Jund's back.

He had not been lashed yet.

Thorne's throat tightened. Artur had saved Jund for him.

But in whipping Jund, there would be no way to avoid hitting the men who stood to either side of him, the ones who had already been beaten. Jund's accomplices would suffer yet again.

You are too weak for this role, his mother's voice whispered in his ear. *You will never be worthy of Artur's throne.*

"Thorne," Artur commanded. "Begin."

Thorne hesitated, overcome with grief at the thought of torturing his childhood friend. What Jund had done was unforgivable, yet Thorne struggled to imagine adding to the pain. Harming someone he had loved.

Lashing his brother, someone who had been as good as flesh and blood for all these years...

But then there was Clan Beran. There was this fortress and its carefully preserved culture—and its future, too. That was the greater good.

And then there was Oda. Jund's treason had almost killed her today.

If Thorne couldn't be strong enough for the clan, then he would never earn their respect and trust. He would never be worthy of their love.

Or hers.

It was this realization that propelled him forward, raising the whip to strike Jund's back.

THORNE WASN'T sure how many times he lashed Jund, nor how long the torture continued. After the whip's first impact, it was almost as though Thorne left his body to its own devices. His movements were automatic, his mind completely blank, his ears incapable of hearing the men's cries for mercy.

Roaring filled his head, and he wasn't sure whether it was his own voice, the voices of the prisoners, or the inexplicable rush he sometimes felt when his heart raced and his emotions overtook him.

Chaos roiled within and without, and he could make little sense of any of it.

It was only when Artur called a halt to the madness and Thorne fully returned to awareness, his limbs trembling as beads of sweat slid down his face and neck, soaking his hair and his tunic. His chest heaved with the exertion, and his ears began to ring, shrill and piercing.

Jund had collapsed against the stone wall, pressing his forehead to it, his back bloody and shredded. All the prisoners were compelled to either stay on their feet or to all kneel at once, lest one of them strangle on the shackle that bound each neck.

"Well done, Thorne," Artur said, signaling for Rynd to take the whip from his hand. "A truly impartial leader leaves his sentiments behind and does what he must. You've proven yourself capable."

Thorne forced himself to hold eye contact with Artur, though an overwhelming weight pressed down on his head and shoulders. He wanted only to look at the floor, to retreat into darkness and never emerge. This wasn't what he had imagined the trials would be. Not at all.

For years, he'd heard stories of feats of strength and battles to the death in the arena. What was happening here was a far cry from those tales.

"Now, we will decide these men's fate," Artur continued. He looked to Tyr, who stood by Thorne's side, arms crossed, a grim expression on his face.

Thorne dared not look to Oda or Iva. Instead, he kept his attention fully on Artur.

"Tyr," Artur said, "this decision is yours. I want to see how you would choose if you were overlord."

Tyr raised his brows, tilting his head in thought. With little hesitation, he asked, "The traitors opposed your marriage to this woman because she's from Iathium?"

"Indeed," said Artur. "And of Clan Mór."

"If we had time for creativity, I would say bring mountain archers to the arena and make a tournament of it," Tyr said, stroking his clean-shaven chin in mock consideration. "That would be quite the spectacle."

"No need for spectacle," the overlord chuckled. "They received enough attention."

"Then what about this?" Tyr began. He clasped his hands

behind his back, slowly pacing back and forth as he surveyed the prisoners, their backs still turned to the room. "Humiliation. Death at the hands of Iva Mór's own city guards."

"No!" Jund growled, jerking as though to turn. His bindings and the shackle around his neck prevented it.

Thorne's heartbeat thundered, a voice in his head echoing Jund's cry—*no, no, no.*

"Even better," Tyr continued, "have the sentries kill the four, then let their leader drag their bodies to his cell. Let them fester beside him while he ruminates on his crimes. Until he begs for his own death at your bride's hands. What better way to welcome her into the clan? Give her the power of vengeance."

Artur's eyes lit, his lips curving into a wicked smile. "Fitting."

Thorne turned in search of Iva and found her standing against the opposite wall, her hand pressed to her mouth. She shook her head, squeezing her eyes shut.

He was thankful her husband-to-be was too preoccupied with Tyr's idea to take notice.

Oda moved to Iva's side, snaking an arm around her shoulders. Gently, she grasped Iva's wrist, shushing her as she coaxed her hand down.

"You mustn't cry out," he heard her whisper in Iva's ear. "It will be all right."

Iva took a few shuddering breaths through her nose, her hands trembling as she gripped Oda's free hand. A tremor wracked her entire body, but then she stood tall, steadying herself.

Thorne wanted to say, *this is what you chose. This is who you are now.* And the same was true of him.

They were going to stand by while Artur allowed sentries of Iathium to execute four of these traitors. This was worse than a traitor's death; it was, perhaps, the most humiliating execution ordered by any overlord in Rodhlan's history. It was shameful for Artur to have approved it, and it brought shame upon his family and the clan.

The Beravakt should have carried out these executions and no one else. To be stripped of this decision was perhaps one of the most degrading things Artur could have done to Thorne.

He knew it, and so did Tyr. And that was why Thorne couldn't openly object.

If all of this was a test of his loyalty, then Thorne would be the picture of loyalty.

Thorne wasn't the only clansman who would have to play along. Iva would get one night, perhaps two, to prepare herself to kill Jund. She would be forced to face not only the man who had led a rebellion because of her, but the rotting corpses of his accomplices.

This gentle woman, whose story Thorne had yet to hear, would be fully initiated into Clan Beran's infamous brutality.

And for the first time, Thorne understood why the people of Iathium spat their name and called them dogs.

If there was any hope for Clan Beran, then he must defeat Tyr at all costs. Thorne must prevail in the trials and go on to make a better name for his clan.

CHAPTER 16

ODA

When it was over, Oda, Thorne, and the rest of Artur's small entourage left Jund behind in the dungeon broken, bleeding, and begging for death.

Every time Oda blinked, she could see the sentries' swords driving between the shoulder blades of each prisoner and through their hearts, one after another, until all except Jund were dead.

His screams followed them all the way back to the main corridor and beyond.

Artur and Tyr paraded at the head of the group, a blood-smattered, somber Thorne trudging behind them. Oda couldn't get his grief-stricken roar out of her head. The sounds he had made as he carried out Jund's lashing had been torturous in themselves.

It was a side of Thorne that Oda had never seen, both vengeful and filled with regret. She hoped Artur had not recognized all the emotions, all the hesitancy, Thorne had displayed back there.

She supposed that if he had, he might have driven Thorne out of the trials by now.

Beside Oda, Iva clutched herself tightly, her knuckles white where she gripped her own arms for support. Her sentries followed them in grim silence, and Mjit and Rynd brought up the rear of the company.

No one spoke; there was nothing worthwhile to say.

When they finally reached the courtyard, Artur clapped Tyr on the shoulder. "Join me for ale in the hall," he said. "You have done well tonight."

Artur surveyed Thorne from head to toe, lip curling in distaste.

He added, "I would ask you to join us, Thorne, but you're covered in blood. Clean yourself up. You'll be summoned in the morning."

"Lord." Thorne bowed his head.

As the group disbanded, Oda found herself alone with Iva and Thorne. The cool night wind whipped Iva's dark curls around her face, and at last, her chin trembled.

"We can escort you to your chamber," Oda said softly. "Would you like that?"

Iva nodded, a tear slipping down her cheek. "Thank you."

In silence, the three entered the winding stone corridor that wound up to the second level, where Iva's guest chamber was located. She opened the door and stepped inside, a grave expression on her face. After a moment of hesitation, she motioned for them to follow.

"What about your guards?" Oda murmured.

"They're drinking with Artur," Iva sighed. "They'll post outside my door overnight, but I don't expect them back for some time yet."

Oda and Thorne exchanged a glance, then followed Iva inside. It was a spacious chamber with ample light. Lanterns were lit and situated evenly around the room, and there were plenty of candles she could light if she wished.

Like all Fortress Hageir's chambers, there was a comfortable bed piled with furs and a bathing room with a large tub. A sheer canopy of delicate gossamer had been hung above the bed, its fabric enveloping the large mattress and cascading all the way to the floor. On the far side of the room, a heavy wardrobe stood, its doors carved with mythical scenes resembling those at the Arthmael's Hall. One door stood ajar, revealing an array of beautiful gowns, soft tunics, and fur-lined cloaks within.

"Cast your silencing spell, Thorne," Oda said absently.

Thorne gave her a puzzled look but did as he was told. Oda's ears adjusted to the new pressure in the room, and Iva rubbed at her own.

Oda turned to Iva then. "Now we may speak freely," she began. "No one outside this room can hear."

"What sort of magic is this?" Iva asked, her forehead creasing.

"It's a spell from Thorne's father," Oda said. "He's a healer in Iathium. I'm sure you know of him."

"The Rí's healer? Yes," Iva said, looking at Thorne again as though for the first time, her eyes widening in recognition. "He's your father?"

"He is," Thorne answered gruffly.

Iva surveyed him closely. "It's hard to see the resemblance beneath all that blood. You can use my bathing chamber if you'd like. We'll send Oda after your clothing."

Thorne looked down at himself, stretching his arms out in front of him. "It is only on my tunic and arms."

"And your face, and in your hair, and in your beard," Oda remarked. "It's everywhere. Don't argue with the lady; I think we all need some quiet time—but perhaps not alone."

"It is not decent," Thorne protested weakly.

"Oh, come on." Oda gripped the sleeve of his tunic and guided him toward the bathing chamber. "No one wants to see *that*. You're perfectly safe here."

The lie slid easily from her lips, but her burning cheeks said otherwise.

"I will bathe," Thorne conceded, "but in my trousers."

She gave his back a little shove as he passed. "Then go do it. You'll smell better, regardless."

He pressed his lips into a thin line as he stepped into the bathing chamber, pushing the door shut behind him. It didn't click, but he didn't bother to latch it, so Oda left it as it was.

When she turned back to Iva, tears were streaming down the older woman's face.

"I can't go through with this," she said, her voice thick with emotion. "I've failed my children already, and I haven't even married him."

Oda stepped forward, clasping Iva's shoulders and guiding her to sit on the side of the soft bed atop the furs. "Tell me why you think you've failed your children."

Iva took a deep breath, steadying herself again. She wiped her cheeks with the back of her hand. "They will need Artur's protection one day. This is how I secure it."

"What do you mean?" Oda narrowed her eyes.

"My husband—" Iva paused again to breathe. "My late husband died on a mission to Iteloria with Rí Corlan. It was four years ago. All I know is that it had to do with my daughter's magic, and perhaps Eremon's, too."

Oda offered her hand, and Iva grasped it before she continued. "Lira doesn't understand her destiny. Her father set her on a path to the archive because he was trying to shield her from it.

"Eremon is aware of what she stands to inherit: Clan Mór's birthright power, which will allow her to see history as it happened. Her grandmother chose her for this destiny, and it is decreed. But Lira doesn't believe magic exists, and revealing the truth to her will take time and patience.

"After news of Gild's death reached Iathium, Eremon arranged a meeting between me and Artur. He believes a match will grant Clan Beran's protection to Lira and Talfryn, in the event the city becomes unsafe for them. I don't understand all that's to come, but I'm trying to trust he has our best interests at heart."

Oda didn't understand. "Can't Eremon just tell Lira about her magic?"

Iva sighed. "You haven't spent much time in Iathium, have you?"

"No." Oda shook her head. "I hear it's awfully backward."

"Magic wielders exist only in secret there," Iva explained. "There is coming a time when these powers will be out in the open again, but we aren't there yet."

"Why wait so long? Surely there's no benefit in letting this drag out."

"Eremon is not yet in his full power," Iva admitted, "and I don't know when that will be. His mother still holds too much sway over the council. Everything he does must be done in secret, and slowly, until the time is right."

"So you're here in hopes that Artur will protect your family if that time comes," Oda breathed.

Inexplicably, she found herself pitying Iva. After seeing Artur's cruelty on full display today, it was difficult to believe that he would have enough compassion for Iva or her children to go out of his way for them. This woman must truly be desperate, to have traded her life to Clan Beran in exchange for such uncertainty.

Iva nodded, her expression resolute. "Yes. But I won't kill someone to be a part of this clan." She wrapped her arms tightly around herself, her voice low and firm. "I don't care what that man did, what crime he committed. I can't drive a dagger into his heart, or whatever Artur thinks he can demand of me."

Oda's heart ached for Iva. "It will only endanger your family more if you go against Artur. Jund will die, regardless of who lands the blow. If it's you, then you will have proven yourself to your future husband and protected your family in the process."

"If I do this, he'll ask it of me again," Iva protested, shaking her head. "How many times will I be forced to take a life to prove my loyalty to this clan?"

"As many as you must," Oda answered grimly. "But I'll be here to see you through it. And so will Thorne. We're healers; we can soothe your feelings. There are remedies that help us overcome the things we must do to defend the fortress."

Oda had taken her first lives as a young guard at the water's edge three years ago, when two invaders had attempted to enter Fortress Halgeir unannounced. She had split one's head with her axe and run the other through with her broadsword. Thorne's father had helped her to recover from the worst of the aftereffects, but she still dreamt of the scene from time to time.

"If you have remedies," Iva said, nodding toward the bathing chamber's door, "he will need them tonight."

It was eerily silent, and Oda realized that she had never heard Thorne fill the tub. At a second glance, she realized that he had not taken a lantern or a candle with him either.

He must be sitting alone in the dark, she thought.

When she turned around, she saw Iva's expression had softened.

"You should go to him," she said in a low voice. "He needs you."

Oda blinked. "I can't. He's to marry."

Now that the trials' pacing had been sped along, the selection would happen sooner rather than later.

Iva confirmed this when she said, "They will announce the names tomorrow."

Her thoughts swirled into a panicked refrain. *No, no, no, no, no. Not yet. Not yet.*

A lump rose in Oda's throat, but she swallowed hard. "Oh. Then you see? I absolutely *can't* go to him now."

Iva leaned near. "No one has to know. It's safe with me. *I* am safe."

"So am I," Oda answered, a lump rising in her throat. "And so is Thorne, no matter what you saw today. He did what he must, as you will. As we all have."

With a shuddering breath, Iva nodded. "Go to him. Take one of my lanterns. I'll knock in an hour; that should be plenty of time before the sentries return."

Oda rose on trembling legs, taking a lantern as she went. Her face burned, and she was too self-conscious to look back at Iva before she quietly entered the bathing chamber and shut the door behind her.

Just as she'd thought, Thorne was sitting in the dry tub, fully clothed. His knees were drawn up, and he was resting his head on his arms.

As her lantern illuminated the small chamber, he looked up, squinting.

"I heard that," he muttered. "So it's tomorrow?"

"Tomorrow," Oda confirmed, the word nearly lodging in her throat.

Thorne sighed. "I told you, this isn't decent," he said, though the strength was sapped from his voice.

"Damn your sense of decorum," Oda chided. It felt good to relax into their natural Brylla cadence again. "My friend needs me."

Thorne stared straight ahead into nothing as she sat on the edge of the tub, near its faucet. Clan Beran's culture might be brutal, but its few true comforts were the envy of Iathium. There was hot, running water throughout the fortress thanks to systems her father had helped Artur perfect a decade ago. She never ceased to feel pride in his work.

Oda set the lantern on the side of the tub and looked down to assess Thorne. At least he had removed his belt, bandolier, and weapons, and had set them aside.

"All right," she said. "You can keep your trousers, but off with your tunic."

She held out a hand expectantly. With a scowl, Thorne peeled off his blood-soaked tunic and shoved it into her hand. Oda tossed it aside, her eyes skimming his muscular torso.

Forcing herself to turn her attention to the faucet, she turned on the warm water, adjusting the lever until its temperature felt comfortable. As the tub began to fill, she perused the soaps and tonics that lined its far side.

"Which do you like best?" she asked, running her fingers along the ceramic containers and beautifully-carved bars of soap.

"It doesn't matter," Thorne mumbled, "since you won't be bathing me."

"And who will?" Oda shot back. "Certainly not you; you had the chance already."

He grunted.

"We're getting the blood out of your hair, off your face, and out of your beard. It's only practical. I can see it, and you can't." To emphasize her point, Oda waved toward the bare wall, where a looking glass should have been hanging. "Besides, you can't meet your future bride covered in gore. So that's that."

"You should be resting," Thorne protested. "You could have died today."

"But I didn't," she said, her stomach doing a flip at the shift in his expression—from stony and distant to tender. Searching. "Which means I'm here to torment you a little longer."

Thorne closed his eyes, sighing quietly. "There's no one I would rather have tormenting me."

Oda smiled, selecting a cleaning cloth and a bar of mild soap that smelled of cedar. Before she wet the cloth, she conjured a golden orb of healing magic in her right hand.

"May I touch you?" she asked softly.

Without opening his eyes, Thorne nodded once. She

extended her arm and pressed the magic against his heart. His skin was warm, the hair that covered his chest soft against her palm.

Beneath her touch, she felt him relax, and he took a long, deep breath.

"Thank you," he whispered.

Oda hummed. "Of course."

She applied soap to the cleaning cloth. "I'm going to wash the blood off your face first. Then you can take the cloth and get it off your arms."

Leaning forward, she reached for him, intending to swipe the cloth over his cheek. But the distance between them was awkward, and there wasn't a comfortable place to sit on the tub's edge that allowed her to reach his face easily.

So Oda shut off the lever and climbed into the large tub with him—fully clothed and unapologetic.

She sat astride his thighs, and his eyes flew open at the contact.

"What are you doing?" he hissed, though his hands rested easily on her hips.

Water soaked up to her waist; the tub hadn't yet filled completely. She shrugged. "I can reach you better this way. Close your eyes."

He did. In silence, she began to wipe the dried blood from his face. His beard was trimmed short, so it was easy to clean, too. At his continued silence, she moved to his ears, neck, and shoulders.

This intimacy was oddly familiar, and she questioned whether it should feel so right to be this close to Thorne. After all, if he won the trials, his path was set. And if Tyr's display tonight had been any indication, then Thorne *must* win. For all of them.

She shoved down the pang of disappointment that rose to her throat. Perhaps a bit more distance would be best.

Oda offered the cloth to Thorne and moved away, pressing her back against the tub's opposite side.

"Your turn," she said, her voice wavering a bit. "You can get your arms and chest."

Thorne nodded, sitting up straighter in the tub. He worked the cloth over his skin in slow swipes, silently clearing away the flecks of blood that still clung to him.

"I don't know about this *duty*," he mused, rinsing the cloth and applying more soap.

"You chose this path," Oda said accusingly. "Can't turn back now."

He grunted. "Tyr can't win. That's certain."

She shrugged a shoulder. "Then there's your answer."

Once he was done, Oda let the water drain, then started a fresh stream from the faucet. She couldn't stand the thought of either of them soaking in water tainted with blood. Either Jund's or the other traitors'.

The tub began to fill for a second time. Thorne tilted his head, giving her a puzzled look as she closed the drain again.

"Your hair," she said, gesturing vaguely toward his head. She grabbed a ceramic cup from the side of the tub, filling it with clean water. "Wet it."

"I know how to wash my hair," Thorne muttered, swiping the cup from her.

Part of its contents sloshed into the tub, and he scowled. Oda couldn't help but snicker. He tilted his head back and dumped the remaining water over his hair.

"Your braids," she said softly, nudging his calf with her foot. "Remember to loosen them."

"Berav's ear," he groaned, looking at the ceiling. "Why must you be so difficult?"

Oda grinned. "It has nothing to do with me. Do you need help taking them out?"

"I don't *need* it," he ventured, "but I don't think I would refuse it."

Again, Oda moved near to him. She sat tall on her knees, gently unbinding the plaits he'd woven into his hair.

Thorne often wore singular braids. Other times, like tonight, he wove one side of his hair up and away from his face. These plaits were more difficult to achieve and took longer to remove, but she had always loved the way he looked when he wore his hair this way.

Oda shivered when his large hands found their way to her hips again, one drifting to her lower back. Thorne's fingertips pressed against the soaked linen of her tunic as she worked.

Oda was so close to him; she could smell the scent of fresh soap on his skin.

This wasn't the first time they'd been so near to one another; after all, they fought in the arena daily. They knew each other's bodies by virtue of combat, but they had never shared space in this way. Not until today.

And no matter how many times Oda tried to convince herself that this nearness was no different than grappling, the more her cheeks heated. The more her heart raced.

This was *nothing* like the arena, and she knew it. And so did he.

They could stop this right now and pretend none of it had ever happened.

Maybe that would be easier than enjoying this closeness for too long. After all, it would never be something they could keep for themselves.

Oda ran her fingers through Thorne's hair then backed off again, handing him the cup so he could rinse and cleanse it. As much as she wanted to do it herself, she knew this overwhelming feeling of desire would only grow.

She couldn't afford to *need* Thorne; he wasn't hers to want, much less need.

But *Berav's ear*, as he liked to say—whoever got him would be a lucky woman.

She sat still against the opposite side of the tub, the water lapping at her stomach, and watched Thorne rinse the last of the soap from his hair. He ran wet hands over his face, swiping the water away from his eyes, and looked at her with a heat in his gaze that set her heart pounding.

From within Iva's chamber, there came a banging on the outer door. Thorne's eyes went wide just before Oda snatched the lantern from the tub's side and blew it out, plunging them into darkness. He withdrew the silencing spell, then recast it inside the bathing chamber alone.

They sat still, straining to listen to what was going on in Iva's room.

"My lord?" Oda was thankful that Iva's lilting, soft voice carried well enough that they could hear.

"I wish to retire with you." It was Artur's voice.

Oda pressed a hand to her mouth to prevent herself from yelping.

"Of course, my lord," they could hear Iva say. "But shall we retire to your chambers? My room feels a bit cool. I'm sure yours are much warmer and more accommodating."

"I have not yet invited you to my chambers," Artur mused.

"Of course; I'm inviting myself," Iva replied. "What say you?"

There was a long silence, hinting at a kiss or a prolonged embrace. Oda cringed; across the tub, she was sure Thorne was doing the same. After an agonizing moment, Artur spoke again.

"Come, my love," he said. "We'll go to my chambers tonight."

"As you wish," Iva said.

A moment later, the outer door of her room clicked shut, and Oda and Thorne were left alone in Iva's tub.

"Mortal *gods*," Oda groaned, and the two of them burst into relieved laughter.

"She must be one, to engage with the likes of Artur," Thorne said quietly. "A mortal goddess, I mean."

"Maybe she is," retorted Oda with a laugh. "After that spectacle today, I can't imagine anyone but *divinity* putting up with him—or climbing into his bed, for that matter."

Thorne sighed heavily. "Today was terrible."

She paused, frowning. "I know."

Silence fell between them. There was so much Oda wanted to say, yet so little that seemed appropriate.

She could apologize for the failed rebellion her sister had been a part of, however indirect. Or the fact that Thorne had been forced to torture Jund. Or she could say she was sorry for frightening him when she'd been injured.

Finally, she settled on saying something infinitely more asinine.

"I'm sorry about the lantern," she said. "We'll have to grope around for drying cloths."

"That's fine," Thorne said. "It doesn't matter."

For a second time, Oda drained the tub. A chill snuck across her skin as the water began to recede. She must have made a sound, because a moment later, Thorne said, "You're cold?"

"A little," Oda admitted.

"So am I." In the dark, he reached out, managing to press a hand to her shin. "Come here."

Beneath the receding water, Oda grasped Thorne's hand. She used it to find her way back to his lap. And in the pitch darkness, her mouth found its way to his.

The kiss was tender and heartbreaking and full of longing. Thorne braced one hand on her hip, cupping her cheek with the other. Oda cradled his face, drinking in the feel of his soft beard, the wet hair that fell over his shoulders, the familiar scent of his skin.

He was so warm, and she pressed herself as near to him as she dared, soaking in his powerful presence and this new knowing of the familiar arms that clung to her.

Oda would never be able to keep this, but how could she give it up? Now that their lips and tongues traced one another, now that their hands wandered, she could see how every step of their journey had been leading them here. Nothing had ever felt so perfect or so destined to happen.

She broke away long enough to say, "You have to win the trials."

He silenced her, slanting his mouth over hers again before he replied, "I know."

A rush of desire swept through her body. "You'll have to marry another."

"I know." Thorne gripped her waist harder, cupping the back of her neck like he had in the healer's chamber.

Their lips met again, but the kiss slowed into something languid and exploratory. Maybe tonight was the only chance Oda would ever have to experience this, so she would savor it. But they couldn't take it any further.

There was no use in hoping to be anything more than friends and fellow warriors. Thorne already knew that.

He broke from her lips, kissing the tip of her nose. "Stay with me tonight," he whispered.

Oda's lips parted in astonishment. If only she could say *yes* without hesitation. But she would never forgive herself if she prevented Thorne from doing his duty for the clan.

"I—I can't," she stammered, her chest aching at the admission. "Don't you remember? You insisted I rest."

"You could rest with me," he coaxed, pressing another kiss to her mouth. "I don't want to be alone."

"Neither do I," Oda admitted, "but these are the trials. Someone will notice. It's going to be tricky enough getting out of here tonight."

Thorne sighed. "Let me try this again: I don't want to be without *you*."

Tears welled in her eyes at his admission. At the gentleness and longing in his voice. She'd believed he only saw her as a friend, but that embrace in the healer's chamber—these quiet moments in the dark—completely shattered that illusion.

For years, Oda had admired Thorne and craved his friendship. The two had always been drawn to one another, although she had often dismissed their closeness as mere duty. *Duty.* She almost snorted at the irony.

Oda had never allowed herself to explore the deeper feelings she harbored for Thorne. She had long since buried those, tucking them safely away, never to be examined. Within the space of a breath, she had unearthed them, undoing the years of effort she had poured into ignoring her desire.

Even though she was still in his arms, she craved this closeness again. Already missed it. It would take every ounce of willpower she had *not* to follow him back to his chamber tonight.

As though reading her thoughts, Thorne tightened his hold. "*Please.*"

Oda closed the remaining distance between them to kiss him once more, brushing her lips gently over his. Thorne skimmed his knuckles across her cheek, then pulled her body flush against him and deepened the kiss. Her heart pounded erratically as a visceral, heated desperation passed between them, and a low groan rumbled deep in Thorne's chest.

A few minutes more, and there would be no coming back from this. There was *already* no coming back for Oda, because she would never be able to suppress her feelings for him again.

Gods, this has to stop. It has to stop now.

Gently—reluctantly—she forced herself to break the kiss. Her body was trembling, and she wanted to weep. "This isn't something we can have. We both know it. You have a duty to the clan, and we've sworn oaths: you to Artur, and I to you."

"Duty." Thorne's breathing was ragged, his voice rough with desire. "I want *you*."

Oda pressed her forehead to his and heaved a sad sigh. "You will always have me as your warrior and your friend. But anything more will be impossible."

CHAPTER 17

THORNE

That night, Thorne didn't sleep.

After he and Oda had gone their separate ways, he had followed the path to his chamber numbly. Once again, he felt as he had in the dungeon: somewhat outside of his body, and not wholly in control of his movements.

Still, he managed to find his way to his chamber, where he sat with his head in his hands until the sun rose.

His father had been right. What had he done to himself by joining Artur's trials?

At the time, he'd been trying to chase away his mother's memory and the exacting voice that still echoed in his mind. In part, he had also made his decision for love of the clan. But in doing so, he had foolishly believed that he could accomplish every feat Artur required.

Thorne had never known that wanting someone could feel this way. Before Oda, he had even believed himself immune to these feelings. Now, he knew that her friendship and trust had unlocked something within him that could never be contained again.

This was why she had been so appalled at his speech about

duty. He played it over and over in his head, now disgusted with himself for having uttered such words.

The privilege of Beran's throne demands great sacrifice, he had said.

Great sacrifice, indeed. If he won these trials, he would sacrifice any chance he might have had to be with Oda. Of course, she had said she would remain by his side—but not in the way he wanted her. Instead, she would always be a reminder of everything he'd given up before he even knew he had it.

Make the treasure forbidden, and it's all he'll be able to think about, day and night, Oda had said.

It was true. She had rejected his offer to join him in his chamber, and already, her absence was driving him mad.

You think I'm like most men, Thorne had boasted, *but I can control my impulses.*

Yet here he sat, alone, because Oda had been the one to control hers. She was duty-bound, and he was scouring his mind for any possible way to be alone with her again.

It was true that Thorne could sacrifice his reputation, perhaps leave the clan altogether, to be with her.

But then he would be handing the throne to Tyr.

That would be infinitely worse than the path Artur was leading them down now. Thorne had chosen to take responsibility for Clan Beran's future, not fully understanding that the overlord had no intention of fulfilling his past promises of glory. Artur's display of brutality, his calculated alliances outside the fortress, and his arrogant performance before the outsiders had shed light on his true intent: to further elevate himself, while simultaneously subjugating the clan.

He laughed bitterly to himself, shaking his head. Once, he had foolishly believed that Artur cared for their people as he did. Now, he knew the truth, but the truth didn't change what he must do.

Thorne was locked firmly into these trials, regardless of what he wanted. *Who* he wanted.

His thoughts drifted back to Oda, and the feeling of her body pressed against his. Her mouth brushing over his own.

Never before had he kissed a woman, much less invited one to his bed. But this was Oda. It had been so easy for the question to escape his lips before he thought twice.

These feelings that had emerged between them were not new; they couldn't be. Maybe they had been there for longer than he'd known, building just beneath his awareness. At the slightest temptation, they had broken the surface with a violence that wrested every practical thought from his mind.

Today. The selection of potential brides would happen today, and he had allowed himself to fall in love with the one person he would never be able to have.

His body shuddered, and he pressed the heels of his hands against his eyes.

Berav, what do I do?

Like always, the prayer would drift into oblivion and be answered with silence. Thorne had thrown enough fruitless pleas into the ether to know. Still, it was instinct to cry out, even if that cry was only a roar in his head.

CHAPTER 18
ODA

Oda dozed fitfully through the night, alternately tossing in her bed and lying still to listen to her sister breathe.

She wanted to be in the room when Cynda awoke; it was the only way she could hope to contain her sister's reaction to the news of Jund. This was one reason why she had turned down Thorne's offer.

Another reason was that she had enjoyed their kisses far too much, and she knew she would not have the strength to tell him no again.

Not when she had to let him go.

She had already imagined all the ways they might couple and all the places in the fortress where they could do so discreetly. In her mind, she had mapped out a myriad of scandalous opportunities.

With Thorne's silencing spell, any place they found privacy would do.

Oda was a trusted member of his ranks. They routinely sought quiet places to converse, to heal, to strategize. It wouldn't be hard to love him, in spite of everything that stood in their way.

Which meant she could not be alone with him again.

Which also meant that perhaps she should reconsider her decision to remain at Fortress Halgeir.

You will always have me as your warrior and your friend. But anything more will be impossible.

She sighed. That had been a lie.

Oda couldn't be *anything* to Thorne at all.

If Thorne was committed to leading the clan one day, then Oda couldn't be his weakness. Eventually, they would be found out. They would inadvertently give themselves away, or someone else would do so for them.

Far from the distraction she might create for him, she could then be used against him.

The last thing she wanted was to be wielded as a weapon against Thorne Beran. She was meant to fight by his side; to be a weapon *for* him.

Her thoughts drifted back to Cynda. How would she explain that Thorne had been forced to beat Jund within an inch of his life? That Iva Mór had been tasked with his execution in just a few days' time?

Exactly how long Iva would have before she delivered the killing blow was uncertain, but Oda knew it had to happen soon. Jund likely wouldn't survive for more than a week or two at most, chained to his dead accomplices. And with his wounds, which would be festering by now, that time would be cut even shorter. It would be a mercy if he simply died before the overlord returned to the dungeon.

Then, Iva wouldn't have to perform the execution she so dreaded—though there would surely be others.

As long as Artur reigned, Clan Beran's people would never escape this brutality. Oda hoped that Thorne would have the strength to change their fate one day, but that future was still a faraway dream. And it would depend on Thorne's ability to withstand the enormous pressure he would endure as heir, and to assume the throne with his empathy intact.

Once this was all over, she and Cynda would move on with their lives. But Cynda would never forgive Oda, nor Thorne. And there would be no real future for the sisters here, regardless.

Because if Oda had to distance herself from Thorne from now on, then what was the point of remaining among the Beravakt ranks? She couldn't watch him be joined to someone else. Not now, and not ever.

And if Cynda would live out her days in misery, unforgiving and forever scarred by the death of her lover, then where would that leave any of them?

There had to be another solution. Maybe Oda was meant to sever her connection to Clan Beran more fully than simply leaving.

She sat up in bed, drawing her knees to her chest. Killing Jund in silence was an option; she could dose him with too much *sjepdraught,* and he would peacefully slip into the after-world without a sound.

But perhaps there were other ways to show mercy.

A plan formulated in her mind, and the next steps suddenly became clear.

By the time Cynda began to stir later that morning, Oda had already arranged traveling packs for both of them. She had prepared her explanation and instructions for Cynda to follow.

With any luck, her sister would listen well and do as she was told.

With a lot of luck, Oda thought bitterly.

Tomorrow was Thorne's show of strength in the arena. He and Tyr would fight to the edge of death. It wasn't a matter of landing a few blows, but of one warrior mortally wounding the other before the fight was called. Although competitors often survived this ordeal, there was a high risk of death in defeat. That depended on the extent of the injuries, and whether a healer could arrive quickly enough to reverse the damage.

In this case, Thorne would be right there. Unless the flow of his magic was somehow staunched because of the fight, he would be able to begin healing Tyr immediately.

The thought of grave harm coming to Thorne, on the other hand, made Oda shudder. Even worse, she wouldn't be present to heal him. She tried to believe that Tyr wouldn't prevail, but after everything that had happened, it was impossible to be sure.

Once the show of strength was completed, then the marriage rite would follow. Oda wouldn't stay to watch it all unfold.

She wasn't willing to exist as a lover behind his wife's back. That would humiliate all parties involved and bring shame to the throne. Whatever Thorne thought he wanted right now, he would never have peace with himself if he took a path of such deception.

He had made his decision, and that was all. There was nothing either of them could do to change it now.

But Oda could take her destiny into her own hands.

She didn't have to remain here and watch disaster after disaster unfold. While Thorne and the descendants of Clan Beran lay in the bed Artur had made for them, she and Cynda would leave for good.

And they would take Jund with them.

Jund didn't *have* to die—at Iva's hands, or anyone else's. He had already been punished beyond his due. This way, Cynda wouldn't lose him. And neither would Thorne.

Even if Jund left Fortress Halgeir forever, simply knowing he was alive would be a balm to Thorne. Eventually.

Saving his friend's life was all Oda could give Thorne now. Then, she would disappear, making his existence as heir easier for them both. If there were other options, she would have loved to know them.

But she could think of none.

CHAPTER 19
THORNE

The arena was full by the time Thorne arrived at its entrance, feeling tired and haggard. He had spent the long hours of the morning mentally preparing for the selection proceedings, lingering over his bindings and battle leathers in hopes that Oda would come to him.

But she had not, and his chest felt terribly hollow at her absence.

In fact, he had not seen any sign of her today, and it was almost noon.

Had yesterday not gone awry, they might have trained together in the arena one last time. But there was a somber heaviness in the fortress today, and no one had gone to the arena floor to train as normal. With the other competitors besides Tyr already eliminated, the anticipated length of ceremonies had been dramatically shortened.

Perhaps Oda was resting, like he'd told her to do.

But something more gnawed at him. He told himself that it was the intimacy they'd shared in the dark the night before; those brief moments that had led to his sleeplessness. But an unsettled current of energy coursed through his body every time he thought of her.

He would understand if she didn't show for the selection. How could he expect her to?

Tyr joined him by the door, his lips twisted into a crooked smirk. "Ready to see them?" he asked, punching Thorne's bicep.

Thorne narrowed his eyes at Tyr. "Step back."

His opponent did no such thing.

"Might as well get used to being close," he said with a confident shrug. "You'll be sharing space with me in the arena tomorrow."

"I will share nothing," Thorne growled.

Tyr rocked back, raising his brows. "Unless you lose. In which case..." He made a show of surveying his surroundings—empty, since everyone was gathered in the arena—before he leaned nearer than before. "I hope Artur put your little warrior girl in the running. I would love nothing more than to—"

Thorne's response was wholly uncontrolled. Before he could think, he had grabbed Tyr by the tunic and slammed him against the arena wall, knocking the breath from him.

Stunned, Tyr went unnaturally still, though he held eye contact with Thorne through the entire exchange.

"Don't speak of her in that way," Thorne growled, "or *any* of my Beravakt."

"Special to you, is she?" Tyr's voice wavered almost imperceptibly, but Thorne detected the fear in it.

Good.

Thorne jolted Tyr against the wall again, letting his head strike the stone. "As are all my warriors."

Tyr barked a laugh. "I'm sure. I see how you watch her."

"*Thorne.*"

Oda's voice caught Thorne off guard, and he let Tyr go, whirling to see her standing behind him.

"Save it for the fight tomorrow," she said, scowling at Thorne. Then, her gaze flicked to Tyr, who sported a wicked grin.

"Please tell me you heard every word," he said, his voice smooth and low. He smirked, raising his eyebrows slightly as his gaze raked over her body.

"I make it my business to ignore everything that comes out of your mouth," Oda spat. "You'll be disappointed to know I'm not among the elect. They're assembled in the war room, I hear."

Thorne's heart sank. He hoped she couldn't read it in his expression.

Oda glanced at Thorne, a warning flashing in her eyes. "If you'll excuse us, Tyr—Beravakt business."

Tyr flashed a salute. "Official business. Of course."

He spun on a heel and strode into the arena, then made his way down the stairs.

Oda craned her neck to watch him go. When she was satisfied he was out of earshot, she grabbed Thorne by the arm and pulled him into the corridor.

When she released him, he crossed his arms and leaned against the wall.

"What's wrong?" he asked.

"I can't stay and watch this," she whispered hastily. "I volunteered for perimeter guard today. You understand."

His heart sank. "Yes."

"Don't forget to use your healing magic," she said. Her voice had taken on a strange cadence, as though she was reciting a memorized speech. "They can't see you falter."

Thorne nodded, noticing for the first time what Oda was wearing. Rather than her usual sleeveless tunic and leather vest, she had donned a long-sleeved tunic with a jerkin belted over it. Her trousers were those she normally used for winter travel, and she wore riding boots rather than the usual soft, broken-in ones she loved for combat.

The roar of the crowd from inside the arena silenced Thorne's questions, and Oda reached into her pocket in haste.

"I made something for you," she said, holding up a smooth, flat stone.

It was an iridescent gray, with a curve worn into it. In the shadows, he thought he could see it shimmer with a hint of gold.

"I imbued it with my healing magic," Oda continued, pressing it into his hand. "But it also collects your worries. Use it in healing and meditation; ask for answers, and they will appear. They're inside of you."

She closed his fingers over the stone, and he could feel the warmth of her power reverberating from it. When she tried to draw away, Thorne caught her hands.

"What's wrong?" he repeated. "Where are you going?"

Oda gave him a pinched smile that didn't reach her eyes. "To the perimeter, like I said."

She pulled her hands free and took a step back. Then another. An ache filled his chest at this small distance, but he didn't reach for her again.

That was when he spied her traveling pack stashed just paces away, and he knew.

Oda was leaving.

"And then where?" Thorne asked, his heart pounding in his ears.

With tears shimmering in her eyes, Oda shook her head. "It's best if I don't tell you where we'll be."

We? She must be taking her sister.

Thorne took a step closer. His own damned eyes had begun to burn. "*Why?*"

"I want—" Her chin trembled, and a tear slid down her cheek. "I want you to remember what we had. What we were.

Because good memories heal. When you use that stone, that's what I want you to think of. Think of me, and think of the good. Promise?"

Another roar rose from the crowd. It jolted Thorne, and suddenly, he wanted to be anywhere but here. He wanted to run with her.

"You have to go," she hissed. "You have to *win*."

Thorne glanced back into the arena for long enough to see that Tyr had already made his way to the floor, where the potential brides would soon be revealed.

When he turned back to plead with Oda once again, she was gone.

CHAPTER 20
ODA

Tears blurred Oda's vision as she slipped through the shadowy fortress, alone and unhindered. Most everyone had abandoned their posts to be in the arena. Anyone who remained would know she was on her way to the perimeter.

After she passed through the dungeon.

Escaping the fortress unnoticed with Jund in tow might have been impossible without the information Cynda had shared with her this morning. If Jund was uncooperative, it might still be. The people here only knew of one way in or out of Fortress Halgeir, but in truth, there were many underground pathways weaving beneath the fortress.

If Jund valued his life, then he would take Oda to one of them.

She adjusted the battle axe she'd strapped across her back and hefted the traveling pack higher on her shoulder. Picking up speed, she wound through the dark stone corridors, encountering few people—and no one who spared her a second glance.

When her sister had awakened, she had been disoriented and forgetful about what she'd known the day before.

Oda had cautiously filled her in on the uprising, the imprisonment—everything that had happened since Cynda had been sleeping. The look on her sister's face had been one of pure contempt.

"Exactly who are you loyal to?" Cynda had demanded. It was a quiet scream that had burned its way down to Oda's soul. *"One moment you're railing against the overlord to me, and the next you're standing by while Jund is tortured. Now you want to betray Thorne and join the traitors. Who are you?"*

"I hardly know," Oda had answered truthfully.

She'd been trying so hard to find belonging among Clan Beran's people that she had lost sight of herself. Somewhere along the way, she had come to value this clan and its acceptance more than her own conscience.

But no matter what Cynda claimed, Oda wasn't betraying Thorne. She would be sparing Jund for him, delaying Iva's first kill, and removing herself from the fray so he could rule without distraction when the time came.

Dark times loomed ahead for Clan Beran. Not because Artur had brought in an outsider to rule at his side, as Iva seemed a good woman.

Instead, it was because Artur had begun the slow erosion of Beran's sovereignty. The more Oda had mulled over the past few days' events, the more disgusted she had become at the way the overlord had allowed sentries to take the prisoners' lives.

There had been so much more to the executions than humiliation.

Artur was opening doors that would allow Iathium's rulers to influence Clan Beran. All the while, the overlord continued to maintain the appearance of supreme authority and clan loyalty.

This was why the rebels had risen up. And Thorne had

admitted that his bid to lead was meant to restore the clan's old ways—its self-sufficiency, its dignity, and the sense of dutiful pride its people had always felt in preserving both.

Oda's pulse drummed as she reached the entrance to the dungeon. She looked over her shoulder, ensuring the corridor was clear before she entered the long, dark pathway that opened into the audience chamber.

She let her vision adjust as she wound her way through the dungeon in search of Jund's cell. Her footfalls echoed in the cavernous hallway, and she regretted having discarded her softer boots in favor of these.

Holding her head high, she ignored the pleas coming from the cells she passed. A sense of relief washed over her when she finally located Jund, who—much to Oda's surprise—was no longer chained to his fellow rebels.

She peered inside his cell and spied him curled against its far wall, his back turned to her. There was a large, gaping wound between his neck and shoulder, which Oda had not caught sight of before. That explained why his arm hung limp.

The wounds Thorne had lashed across his back were festering, and he had not been given a change of clothing. Oda shook off the memory of Thorne with the whip in his hand and paused by the heavy iron door.

Jund sensed the movement and turned his head slowly, wincing in pain when he couldn't manage to look at the door. "Who's there?"

As quietly as she could, Oda took the heavy iron keys from her pack and found the master key that unlocked the cells. The Beravakt's elite members were all entrusted with dungeon keys, as were the healers. Although she had made her decision, a rush of nerves washed over her at the thought of betraying the overlord's trust.

But it was too late to turn back now.

Oda opened the door to Jund's cell and slipped inside, pushing it shut behind her.

Again, Jund tried to turn. This time, he managed to lay eyes on her, and he sneered. "Leave me."

"If you value your life, you will not speak," Oda said quietly. "I'm going to close the wounds on your back."

"Why? So the *sjivoc* can open them again?" His lids were heavy with fatigue, his gaze fogged with pain. "Or better yet, your general."

"*Quiet*, or I'll do it myself," she growled.

Jund's gaze flicked from her boots to her face, and he faced the wall without another word.

Oda knelt on the stone floor of the cell, setting her pack aside and removing the healing balms and herbs she had brought. Making quick work of healing would patch up Jund's wounds enough so that he could travel. His back would scar, but at least the whip's marks would be closed.

She cut away Jund's shredded tunic. He tensed, hissing in pain as she worked slowly to remove it, applying balms to moisten the fabric that stuck to the oozing wounds.

"Why are you doing this?" he asked in a low voice.

"Cynda said you know another way out of here," Oda whispered. "We're going on a journey with her, you and I."

Jund grew still. Oda conjured an orb of golden healing magic between her palms and passed it over his back. He relaxed visibly as the magic spread, then sank into his skin. The wounds began to close, so she conjured another orb and repeated the process.

"You would help us?" he said quietly.

Oda nodded. She might not be able to help herself and Thorne now, but she didn't have to sit by and watch Jund and her sister ripped from one another. It was too cruel; all of this was.

For a quiet moment, Jund peered at her in the dark. Then, he spoke again.

"There are five ways out, besides the main entryway," he said, his deep voice almost inaudible. "Caverns. Catacombs. The overlords believed they would be forgotten if enough generations were lied to."

"I see."

"Their existence puts the fortress at risk from invaders," said Jund, "and few understand that."

It made sense; hidden entrances would remain unguarded. Oda guessed that they weren't widely known outside the fortress, though. She assumed that otherwise, invaders might have already tried to use them.

But the threat could never be from armies spilling into the fortress. Catacombs could only accommodate so many people, so it would be a fool's errand for any leader to send troops into the fortress that way.

No; this meant spies might one day be able to come and go quietly, with no one the wiser.

As Artur relaxed Clan Beran's traditional sentiments and welcomed more outsiders into the fortress, their risk of infiltration would be greater. The clanspeople would grow more and more comfortable with unfamiliar faces, and over time, they would ask fewer questions.

Or perhaps none at all.

"Tell me what you're thinking," Jund pressed.

"It's not safe," Oda said softly.

She hadn't meant to voice her thoughts about the fortress itself, but she hoped Jund would interpret her answer as, *you are not safe to tell.*

But Jund scoffed quietly. "No. And now you understand."

Oda sniffed but didn't respond.

"Don't you wonder why your sister never told you?" Jund asked.

Oda huffed a breath, disbelief sweeping through her. How long had Cynda known about all this? Had her sister really distrusted her so deeply all this time?

"If I had taken the throne, I would have told the people," he continued. "I would have posted guards at every hidden entrance. I would have secured Fortress Halgeir."

"Why didn't you just enter the trials?" she said.

"I could not have defeated Thorne," Jund answered.

"At least there would have been an understanding, where there is none now," Oda retorted, shaking her head. "You wouldn't have faced him as an enemy."

"Perhaps not. But impulsivity is my greatest weakness," Jund scowled. "As evidenced by where we now sit. Those men died because of me."

As she began to heal his wounded shoulder, he turned his head toward her again. "It seems you're similarly afflicted."

"With impulsivity? No," Oda ventured, "more like decisiveness. Decisions have been made that can't be taken back —by all of us. I had to decide what I wanted to do about that."

Jund considered this for a moment, then said, "I never thought you would leave his side."

Oda exhaled. "Neither did I."

"What will you do?"

"Go to my family on the coast," she said. "Try to learn more about my father's culture—understand his story a little better."

"I can tell you what I know."

Oda lost her grip on her magic. It flared abruptly, then dissipated. "How do you—"

"About the deal he made with Artur," Jund said.

Hope surged through her, followed by a heavy sense of dread.

"*What*?" she hissed.

Jund held up a finger to silence her. Then, he lowered his

voice until she could scarcely hear it. "And I will tell you once we've reached the catacombs."

ODA AND JUND crept through the dungeon's dark corridors together, making their footfalls as light as possible. His right arm was still visibly weakened.

She'd been able to knit the muscle and sinew back together, to a point, and the wound was closed. But there hadn't been time to heal it properly. Once they made camp for the night, Oda would work on it more.

She explained her plan in hushed tones as they moved. Oda would get Jund as far as one of the hidden exits, and he would wait for her there. Then, she would fetch Cynda, who would be waiting for her in the courtyard. The three of them would follow the underground tunnels until they reached the outlet into the meadowlands, then disappear into the wilderness.

Oda planned to trace a path east, then southward toward Rodhlan Ridge. It would be easier to travel through the mountains discreetly than to try to cross the open meadowlands. In the wide expanse of grasses and softly rolling hills, they were likely to be spotted. But in the mountains, there would be plenty of places to hide, fresh water to drink, and wildlife to hunt.

They would only have hours to reach safe shelter, if even that long, before anyone in the fortress realized they were gone.

To maintain pretense, Oda believed Artur would send a search party through the conventional entry point near the gorge. Taking dinghies downriver to the meadowlands would delay any Beravakt who came looking for them, and by then, they would be clear of the clan's territory.

Not that territorial bounds would keep Artur from coming after them, of course.

They had moved into the depths of the fortress, on the other side of its dungeon, before Jund stopped her. He gestured toward several large barrels that sat against the wall, stacked high with crates.

"This is the entrance that will take us due east," he explained.

Pressing his back against one of the barrels, he tried unsuccessfully to move it. Oda joined him, and together, they used their weight to slide the barrels aside. Behind them lay a darkened passageway. Damp, cool air from the cavern beneath rushed up to slither across Oda's cheeks.

"I'll wait just inside there," Jund said.

"You're to go ahead if we can't make it back," she replied. "Don't stay here for longer than an hour."

He frowned. "And if we're separated?"

"Try to make it to the foothills east of Acton's Cove," Oda answered. "There's plenty of natural shelter near there, and not many travelers. If you have to wait for us, at least you'll be safe."

She removed her traveling pack, fished out her keys, and pressed the bag into his hands.

"Take this with you. There's a few days' worth of food inside, and a flask for your water. Fill it as soon as you can," she instructed.

Oda almost whirled to go, but then she remembered Jund's promise back in the dungeon.

"We don't have much time," she said. "You said you would tell me about my father's deal."

"I don't know much," Jund hedged, "except this: Your father traded a valuable weapon to Clan Beran in exchange for Artur's lenience. It's one of Clan Énna's most carefully-guarded secrets, yet he betrayed it for you."

She drew in a harsh breath. "What weapon?"

He nodded toward the heavy barrels they'd moved. "It's in

those. They're positioned all over the fortress, at every hidden entrance."

Oda was puzzled. These barrels and crates should have been filled with grain and salted meats the clanspeople stored for winter. "Papa knew nothing about weapons. He was a craftsman; he helped Artur refine the water system here."

"Did you never wonder why your father couldn't share that knowledge with Iathium? With the other clans?" Jund leaned nearer, speaking rapidly. "It was because Artur made your father swear oaths to him alone. He targeted your father for power and political gain. Why else do you think you and your sister received such favor?"

Oda's head spun. Never once had she speculated about what Artur had demanded of Uden. Instead, she had been fixated on her own feelings of inadequacy, and her longing to fit in. Their family had dutifully assimilated, following the overlord's decrees to the smallest detail and leaving everything behind.

Besides his surname and ancestral identity, she had not stopped to question what else her father might have given up —who he might have *betrayed*—to secure a place for them here.

But Uden Beran had betrayed his very *clan* for a place among his wife's people. Unbidden rage scorched her cheeks. How could her father do this to his family—his clan? Why had belonging in this fortress been so important to him?

She tried and failed to calm her racing thoughts. If she and Cynda were going to follow through with their plans to flee, then Clan Beran, with its access to Énna's secrets, would become infinitely more dangerous to her father's birth clan than she'd ever thought possible.

Perhaps if Oda, Cynda, and Elda took the information to Clan Énna's elders themselves, they might beg forgiveness on Uden's behalf. After all, his betrayal was not theirs. Still, they risked making themselves enemies of two clans. Then, Oda's family would truly belong nowhere.

It was a risk she might have to take.

"Tell me about the weapon," she said through gritted teeth.

"It's a powder—the exact antithesis of Clan Énna's water magic," Jund answered. "Fire powder, only worse than fire. It creates a blast that can bring down caverns."

And many, many warriors, Oda thought, dread weighing her down.

She had already hefted one of the smaller crates down from the top of a barrel and pried the lid open. Sure enough, there was an iridescent powder the color of ripe plums inside. It smelled of ash and spice.

"Throw as much as a spark into one of those crates, and you'll collapse this entire passageway," Jund said quietly. "It's powerful enough to rival even the most seasoned magic wielder."

Oda carefully replaced the lid. "And no one knows of it?"

"Almost no one," Jund confirmed. "There's a cache, too—enough to close every remaining entrance to Halgeir."

Clan Beran's people had been systematically taught that Fortress Halgeir was safer with fewer entrances. Safety from invasion was how Artur had justified closing many of the old known tunnels that led in and out. Now, it made more sense.

Bile rose in Oda's throat. "He would lay siege to his own people to maintain control?"

No one in, and no one out.

"Yes," Jund answered gravely. "His bringing outsiders in is a misguided attempt to thwart the need for extreme measures. He sees friendship with Iathium as more important than forti-fying this place further."

"Then we're wise to leave," she said, though her gut told her to race back to Thorne as quickly as she could. He needed to know this, all of it, if he was going to protect their people.

Jund nodded. "We've been here too long. Bring Cynda back here quickly. I'll go on ahead of you if I must."

"Move cautiously," Oda urged, taking a step back. "Your wounds are still wounds, just not as severe as before. Take care."

His expression was somber. Before he disappeared into the shadows, he said, "Thank you."

ODA MOVED AS QUICKLY as she dared through the fortress—sometimes trotting, sometimes sprinting down long stretches of empty corridor.

Judging by the sun's position in the sky as she emerged into the light, she had been with Jund for twice as long as she'd predicted. She prayed that Cynda had stuck to the plan to wait for her in the courtyard.

But when Oda arrived there, it was empty, and Cynda was nowhere to be found.

People were beginning to stream out into the corridors from the direction of the arena, so the selection must be over. Oda didn't want to know who Thorne's potential brides were going to be.

That didn't matter, and curiosity would do her no good.

Right now, she must focus on the task at hand.

She forced herself to take a steadying breath and pushed in the direction of their chamber. Maybe her sister had decided to wait there instead.

In her haste, she nearly ran headlong into Rynd, who grasped her shoulders and shook her.

"Where were you?" he demanded. "Thorne said the perimeter, but you weren't there."

"I had to relieve myself," she lied.

Rynd rocked back and scowled. "So you came all the way back into the fortress to do it?"

"Yes," she said, hoping her voice sounded clearer than it felt, "because of my cycle."

Rynd paled. "Oh, I—"

"Don't look at me like that," Oda snapped, relieved he appeared to believe her. "If you hadn't been so demanding, I wouldn't have had to say it. These things happen, and it's unfortunate when you're unprepared, if you take my meaning."

"Berav's ear," Rynd grumbled, jerking his head in the direction of the arena. "You're needed. Follow me."

Berav's ear, indeed, Oda pleaded silently. *Please hear me, if you never listen again. They know what I've done. Just, please—keep Cynda out of this. Protect her from my foolish ideas.*

Her skin grew clammy, her palms were sweating, and her heartbeat reverberated through her body. For several beats, she didn't trust herself to speak again.

But she finally worked up the nerve to ask, "What's happening?"

"They didn't tell me," said Rynd. "All I know is you're to meet with the overlord."

Terror gripped Oda, and she nodded shakily.

She followed Rynd into the empty arena and down the wide steps to the floor. On the way across the training floor, she spotted Tyr, who grinned broadly when he saw her.

As he passed, he moved so that her shoulder struck him. When she whirled to bark at him, he gave her a mocking bow.

"I'm sorry, *sister*," he said with a smirk. He raised his brows, as if pleasantly surprised. "Has a nice ring to it. Wish me luck tomorrow? I never fancied myself worthy of Cynda, but if *she* is the prize Artur wishes me to receive, I will gladly accept."

Oda faltered as his full meaning sank in.

Cynda had been chosen as one of the heir's potential brides.

With a roar, she turned and sprinted toward the war room,

shoving her way through the remaining Beravakt warriors who were gathered at the mouth of the arena floor. Rage pounded through her veins, and she was ready to draw her weapons until the sight of Artur stopped her short.

He was standing in the doorway to the war room, arms crossed, as though he'd been waiting for her for quite some time.

"You summoned me, lord?" Oda demanded in a low voice.

Artur blinked slowly, lazily, as if they had all the time in the world to stand here in this corridor, facing off.

"Inside," he said, moving aside for Oda to enter.

The long stone table was empty, save for Iva and a trembling Cynda, whose lovely face was stained with tears. She glanced at Iva, whose expression clearly said, *be careful.*

Artur bolted the door behind him and turned to Oda, Cynda, and Iva.

"It seems you were swallowed by the crowd, Oda," Artur said. "Pity you were absent. Families were expected to approach the dais with their daughters during the selection. As you are Cynda's only family at present, you should have been there."

Oda glanced at her sister again, whose eyes had welled with fresh tears.

"I've been unwell today," she answered cautiously, though she wanted to cut Artur down where he stood. "It's improper to elaborate in the company of men."

"Oh," Iva breathed. "We certainly understand."

"We do *not* understand," Artur snapped. "Sit."

Oda did as he commanded, carefully taking a seat across from Iva. Artur presided over the table, leaning down and pressing his fingertips against the stone surface, as though planning for battle.

Where is Thorne? she thought mournfully. It felt so strange for Artur to tower over her this way, like a controlling father demanding submission.

"If it's any comfort, my dear, Oda *was* present during the ceremony," Iva said. "I spied her in the audience, near the back."

"Then you would be the only one," Artur replied.

"Perhaps the crowd made it impossible for her to come down."

His eyes narrowed, and he shook his head, refocusing on Oda. "What was your involvement in Jund's treason, Oda *Énna*?"

Oda flinched. "My lord, I wasn't involved."

Artur slammed a palm against the table. "But you had *knowledge*."

"She did not," Cynda protested, though her voice was weak and gravelly from crying. "I told you."

"What is this, Cynda?" Oda sat up straighter, working her expression into one of disbelief.

"Your sister was seen with Jund in the days leading up to the rebellion," Artur sneered.

"Your pardon, lord, but they worked together in the gardens," Oda protested.

"It's true, Oda. I already confessed." Cynda turned back to Artur. "She had nothing to do with any of this, my lord. I swear."

"And why would she?" Iva asked softly, watching Oda carefully. "Oda has been a loyal warrior, from my understanding. She serves Thorne well among the Beravakt."

Oda swallowed. "Lord, Cynda can't help who she loves, but she's no traitor."

"Yet a fitting punishment is in order," Artur said, "which is why we're here."

Cynda stared at the table. Whatever treason Artur thought her capable of, he had no idea what Oda herself had just accomplished. And when he found out that Jund was missing, all hell would break loose.

Oda had to hold herself together. Once they were free from this room, she and Cynda would find a way to follow Jund. It was their only chance of escape.

"Did you include Cynda in the selection to punish her, lord?" Oda asked. Keeping her tone calm was a battle. "It was my understanding that our father bargained with you to keep us out of it."

Artur recoiled almost imperceptibly, but swiftly recovered. "Until your sister fraternized with traitors, that was true. She has forfeited any standing agreement."

Then you should relinquish the fire powder, Oda thought, though she dared not say it aloud.

"I'm sure our mother would object," Oda replied.

Iva shot her a look that said, *hush.* But it was too late.

Artur scowled. "In her absence, you're the family representative. If your sister withdraws from the selection, she will face a traitor's fate. Is that what you wish, Oda?"

"No, lord," Oda said. Her entire body trembled with barely-contained rage.

"If you want her to live, then you'll accept the punishment I've chosen," Artur continued. His eyes lit with ill-contained glee as he said, "Since she fancies herself an overlord's wife, that is what she'll be.

"Whether Thorne or Tyr prevails, the victor will marry your sister, and she'll be bound to this clan forever."

Oda's breathing was ragged, and she ground her teeth. Her palms itched to draw her axe, but she forced herself to remain still, pinning her hands beneath her thighs.

He leaned down until his nose almost touched Oda's as he seethed, "If either of you tries to stop this, or if you reveal the secret before five years have passed, I will wipe your entire family from the continent. Do not defy me."

CHAPTER 21
THORNE

The din of the Arthmael's Hall overwhelmed Thorne.

From the moment he'd seen Cynda in the line of potential brides, he had hardly comprehended anything anyone said or did. Artur's lips had moved, yet Thorne had not understood a word. The crowd had cheered, yet the cacophony had not once cut through the panicked roar in Thorne's head.

Oda had said that she and Cynda were leaving.

She must not have reached her sister in time.

The women would have been taken from their chambers early that morning. All of them should have been in the arena before the proceedings. Yet, Oda had met him outside the door and told him they were leaving.

Did that mean she was still here in the fortress?

Thorne didn't know; he and Tyr had been moved to the hall immediately afterward, where they'd been bombarded by clanspeople who wanted to watch them goad one another.

There was something deeply wrong about all of this.

At Thorne's side, Tyr whooped and guffawed, slamming his

empty flagon against the table and shouting for more ale. They'd been forced to sit one level below the high table, where Artur and Iva would dine when they arrived.

On the tier below, the seven potential brides had been given seats, some of whom craned their necks to ogle Thorne and Tyr, and none of whom he recognized, save Cynda.

Had he been so absorbed in his duties as a warrior and guard that he no longer knew his people?

Yes. Even more infuriating, Tyr knew every one of them by name.

And he seemed especially keen to watch Cynda's every move.

The hair on Thorne's arms stood on end as his gaze flicked between the two. Cynda sat hunched and unmoving, staring at the table. She had arrived with the last of the thinning crowd, with Oda still nowhere in sight.

Had Oda decided to leave regardless?

Thorne's heart sank. Surely, that wasn't the case.

He found himself watching the doors for her arrival as the first hour dragged by. In the brief moments when he wasn't paralyzed by panic, he thought of their stolen kisses in Iva's chamber. There would never be a chance to experience that again—never an opportunity to explore it further.

Oda had been appalled at the idea of a new husband and wife being separated for five years, but five years was a mercy compared to this.

For Thorne and Oda, this separation would be forever.

The realization ignited a visceral, all-consuming ache in his chest. His breathing constricted further, and his awareness narrowed to the tightness building in his muscles and the near-overpowering urge to flee.

He'd never known this kind of devastation.

Not when his mother had died. Not when Jund had

betrayed their friendship—and their clan. Only now that he had committed himself to Clan Beran's throne was it clear that he'd made the wrong choice.

With trembling fingers, he felt for the place in his bandolier where he'd slipped the gray stone Oda had given him. It was tucked snugly behind his dagger blade, and he slid it out, pressing it between his thumb and forefinger. He closed his eyes, inhaling deeply as the healing magic she'd imbued into the stone soaked into his fingertips.

When he opened his eyes, Oda was standing in the hall's doorway, as though he had summoned her.

She'd brought up the rear behind Artur and Iva, who were already halfway to the high table. Everyone in the hall rose for them, bowing their heads reverently as they passed. The energy of the room buzzed with unrest, however; after the rebellion, the whole of the clan was careful to display only loyalty.

Rather than coming any further, Oda had stopped by the doors, and her eyes were fixed on Thorne.

The emotion in her expression mirrored his feelings so perfectly, he almost jumped from the table to go to her. But under Artur's heavy scrutiny, he could do no such thing.

Instead, he squeezed the stone in a vise-grip as his fellow clanspeople settled back into their seats.

It seemed that Oda noticed the movement, for she peered at his hand briefly before looking back at his face. Slowly and almost imperceptibly, she shook her head, then turned her attention to the remaining seats on the floor.

She slid onto a bench at Rynd's side and was served a pheasant and flagon of ale, yet she sat on her hands and didn't touch her food.

Thorne sank back into his seat, his limbs suddenly as heavy as his heart.

Throughout the meal, Thorne watched Oda. She didn't

speak or eat. Instead, she stared blankly past the warriors around her, never truly present.

A drunken Tyr shoved against him, sloshing warm ale onto Thorne's side. "What if you win, and it's the sister?" he drawled. "Big mess."

Thorne's lip curled as Tyr laughed. "Bury yourself in ale. You're halfway there already."

"I celebrate now," Tyr replied. "You won't win, so there's nothing for you to worry about. I'll take the sister, and you can have Oda. If you live, we'll be brothers."

"I will kill you," Thorne said through gritted teeth.

"Who's the traitor now?" Tyr raised a brow, then raised his flagon. "I'm going to tell."

He sounded like a child in the courtyard.

"If I win the day," Tyr slurred, leaning so close that Thorne could smell the reeking ale on his breath, "I'll make this clan rich. In a year's time, you won't recognize Fortress Halgeir. We'll have more wealth than even the Rí could dream of—gold and silver and jewels."

Thorne snorted, scanning the hall for the hundredth time. "And how will you do that?"

He didn't care enough to form a proper question. Tyr was simply bragging more than usual, owed to the untold amount of drink in him.

"Ah, I'll not give that away," Tyr replied, his voice swallowed by the flagon. "Let us say the overlord harbors secrets that strengthen us in... unnatural ways. And let us say that he believes himself the sole custodian of those secrets."

Thorne sat rigid in the heavy wooden chair as Tyr pushed back his own and raised the flagon. The faster he could rid himself of Tyr, exit the hall, and find Oda, the better.

"To Artur!" Tyr shouted. "More ale!"

"To Artur!" the hall echoed.

In unison, they began a rhythmic drumming, beating fist

and flagon against the heavy wooden tabletops as the women and ale-maidens made their rounds, refilling flagons, taking away empty plates, and replacing them with more food.

Round after round they went, drinking and eating and cheering when there was nothing here worth cheering for.

CHAPTER 22

ODA

Only after Tyr had plied Artur with enough ale to get him singing did Oda feel safe enough to leave the hall.

The crowd was beginning to thin, and Artur's attention was now consumed by Tyr. Several of the Beravakt and two or three of the bridal candidates had also ventured to the second-tier table where the opponents sat.

Thorne was stone-still, his jaw clenched as he stared out toward the courtyard.

It was as close to freedom as any of them would ever get, Oda thought mournfully.

Everything would be over soon. Once Artur discovered that Jund was gone, for it was only a matter of time, he would give a traitor's death to Oda and Cynda. Then, he would hunt down their family until their bloodline was wiped out.

Elda. Rune. Their uncles and cousins. All of them would die, and Oda was to blame for it.

She rose slowly, leaving her untouched plate behind. Someone might have called out to her, but she ignored them, trudging heavily into the moonlit night alone.

On the way out, she encountered two of Iva's sentries who barely paid her any mind as they passed in haste. They must have been worried they had missed dinner, she thought, for they moved at a clip. Shrugging it off, she headed for the arena.

Buzzing energy coursed through her body, setting her on edge.

She needed the outlet of the training floor, even if she was alone. If this was her final night as one of the Beravakt, then she would soak it in.

It was all she had left.

When she reached the arena floor, she stepped out onto the familiar packed dirt. The expansive space was completely empty. Of *course* it was, because the selection ceremony had taken place today.

She stopped for a moment, grinding the toe of her heavy boot into the dirt and contemplating what to do next. The Beravakt must have cleared the floor of the familiar training equipment last night, when she was wounded.

Or perhaps while she and Thorne hid together in the dark.

A violent wave of grief rushed up through her entire body, from her feet all the way to her face. It pulsed and twisted in her gut, but she tried to fight against it as she drew her sword and assumed a fighting stance.

With several deep breaths, she steadied her trembling limbs.

She didn't need the training dummies or the leather bags to pummel; she could practice her footwork and her sword form. That would work.

Oda raised her sword into position and sank into a low stance. She blinked, and the memory of Thorne was advancing on her, his sword raised to strike downward.

And then she began to move.

Block. Counterstrike. Block. Strike.

Oda lost herself in the movements, her muscles burning as

she built momentum. In her memory, in her heart, she sparred with Thorne. Strike by strike, she powered through the drills that had become so familiar to her.

Had she known that she would never face Thorne in this arena again, she would have challenged him one last time.

Sweat and tears mingled on her skin before she finally stopped, panting hard, the evidence of yesterday's injury finally rearing its head. With a shaking hand, she tried to conjure an orb of healing magic to apply to her aching side.

But when all she could think of was her magic mingling and flaring with Thorne's, the dull gold winked out.

She howled with rage, throwing her sword to the arena floor. It clattered to the dirt. Oda drew in another breath and screamed, the sound primal and painful and raw.

When her voice was in shreds, she collapsed into a keening cry, hitting her knees and bowing over onto the floor. She pressed her cheek to the floor and let her tears wet it. Dirt turned to mud against her skin, and she wasn't sure how long she lay crumpled there before she heard footsteps approach.

A familiar pair of soft leather boots came into view, much larger than her own. When the general reached her sword, he kicked it toward her, letting it skitter across the dirt until it stopped just within her reach.

"Pick it up," Thorne said.

His voice lacked its usual fighting edge. Instead, it was filled with compassion. Regret. Grief.

Oda reached out and wrapped her fingers around the hilt, then pulled herself to her feet. When she turned to face Thorne, he was frowning, his eyes glassy. She rolled her shoulders, noting that he'd drawn his own sword as well.

"You relinquished your blade," he said with a disapproving glare.

She closed her eyes, taking a deep breath before she answered, "I'm not worthy of it."

Thorne took a step closer. "You are the worthiest."

Oda shook her head. "When you learn what I've done, you will no longer think so."

He lowered his blade and sheathed it again, tilting his head. "And what is it you've done? What else has happened?"

What else. She almost laughed.

"I can't tell you," she replied, her chin trembling. "I care for you too much. I-I can't put you in danger."

"Is that why you wanted to leave?"

She dipped her head. "In part."

His voice dropped so low, she could barely hear it. "And you wanted to save—"

"But I couldn't," Oda interrupted, her voice thick with emotion. "It was too late. I was too late, and now we're going to die."

Thorne closed the distance between them in two strides, stopping short of reaching for her. He studied her face, alarm flashing in his eyes. "War room. Now."

Oda made a sweep of the arena, scanning for flashes of movement in the dark, for stragglers who might have hung behind the crowd or lurkers in search of a scandal. When she was satisfied they were alone, she nodded, then followed Thorne back to the dark room where Artur had torn her hope apart mere hours before.

Once he'd closed the door and cloaked them in silence, Thorne lit one of the lanterns Artur had left on the stone table.

They sat across from one another, keeping a terse distance that made Oda ache to be near him. Out on the arena floor, she had almost embraced him, but her fear of being caught had outweighed the urge.

Cynda would marry him tomorrow. She couldn't stand in the way of that. It was the best-case scenario, if Jund wasn't discovered missing first.

"Oda, why do you think you're going to die?"

She savored the sound of her name on his lips. "Before I speak, you must understand that I have good reasons for my decisions. I thought leaving was the best choice. You could marry and rule in peace, without me to disturb you. *Especially* now that my sister--"

"But Cynda is one of seven," Thorne interrupted. "She may not be chosen."

"You don't understand. Artur *already chose* her," Oda said. "He told us himself. She's going to be your wife."

Thorne paled, going still. Slowly, he shook his head. "No. No one in the clan is to know, not even the families."

"This time was different, Thorne." Her throat was still raw and sore from screaming in the arena. "He's punishing her for being involved with Jund."

He just sat there, stunned, looking as though he might be sick.

Finally, he said, "So I truly *must* win. I wouldn't want her bound to Tyr."

"There's more," she said softly, "but I'm not sure where to st—"

A scuffling outside the door caught her ear, and she pressed her lips shut. Voices spoke in hushed whispers outside. Thorne froze, too, and together, they strained to listen.

"What's happened, Edmun?" Iva's panicked voice was muffled on the other side of the door.

"Prisoner escaped," a male voice said. His voice carried the refinement of Iathium—one of the sentries, Oda guessed. "Wren went to do what you'd asked, and he was gone."

"*What?*" Iva cried.

"*Hush*—in here," the sentry hissed. He rattled the door, but it was locked, and Oda could hear him swear. "Can't open it."

"There's a light inside," another male voice said. "Someone's in there."

Thorne's brow creased with concern as Oda rose, grabbing the lantern. "Stay here," she whispered.

He shook his head, a panicked look in his eyes.

"Trust me. Get behind the door—I'm going out."

He couldn't be caught down here with Oda, or get involved with whatever was happening among the city folk. But *she* could intervene.

Crossing to the door, Oda cracked it open quietly and peered out. A wide-eyed Iva and two of her sentries, both unarmed, whirled to face her, as though they had been readying to leave.

"It's just me," Oda whispered. "What's happened?"

The color drained from Iva's face, and she shook her head, backing away a few paces. "Nothing. Don't worry."

"You sound worried," Oda hedged.

Iva and Wren exchanged a glance. There was a long silence. Finally, Iva's shoulders sagged, defeated.

"I have a feeling you already heard why," Iva said slowly, "and after what happened in this room tonight, I think you'll help me. Do we have an understanding?"

Oda had been so enraged at Artur during the exchange that she hadn't taken note of Iva's reaction. Now, it was clear that Iva had also been unsettled by him.

She raised her lantern and jerked her chin in the direction of a chamber opposite the war room. "In here. Quickly."

Oda led Iva and the two sentries into the dark chamber, then shut the door behind them. Unlike the war room, which was used for planning, strategy, teaching, and training, this room was used to store and maintain weaponry and training equipment. It smelled of dirt and freshly-oiled leather.

She prayed that Thorne would stay put across the corridor until she could find out what was happening.

Iva's expression was grim. Wary. "Artur is asleep in his

chamber, drunk on ale," she said. "The warriors are still drinking in the hall and likely will be until morning."

Oda pursed her lips, raising her chin. "These are the trials, after all. Someone has to celebrate them." She didn't bother to hide the bitterness in her voice. "It's also convenient if you're up to something."

How true that was.

"Edmun sent Wren to look in on Jund," Iva continued in a hush, "because I wanted to end things quietly. Do you understand my meaning?"

Relief swept through Oda, though she tried not to show it. "I do."

"But Jund is gone without a trace." Iva crossed her arms, straightening. "The cell door was left unlocked, so we believe someone within the ranks let him out. I had hoped to avoid wielding the blade myself, but if there are more traitors among us, I doubt that's possible."

"It's also possible that whoever did it meant no harm to the clan, but hoped to prevent more bloodshed," Oda said before she could stop herself.

Iva's gaze sharpened. "Might the culprit have been absent from this afternoon's proceedings?"

"I'm not sure, my lady," Oda answered in a shaky voice, "since you, yourself accounted for everyone who should have been there. That is, if I recall correctly."

They held one another's gaze steadily, until Iva exhaled and gave her a slow nod. "We're going to need a very good story." Leaning closer, she murmured, "I understand his lordship fears the River Plague."

"Everyone fears that," Oda replied carefully. "It's horrible; I survived it as a child."

"As did I," said Iva.

"I heard there was a fever in the fortress last year, but Artur believed it was plague," Edmun mused. "He and his wife locked themselves in their chambers for a fortnight, but she took ill anyway, and she died."

Oda shifted uncomfortably, pressing her lips together tightly. How had *that* story spread beyond the Beravakt?

"If you're sworn to secrecy, you need not break it," Iva said softly. "To me, the story rings true."

Despite her words, Iva, Edmun, and Wren watched Oda expectantly, as though they believed she would reveal more. Oda studied their faces in turn, her confusion and apprehension mounting.

She finally settled on asking, "Why are we speaking of plague?"

"How does Clan Beran dispose of its dead?" Iva asked. "I've heard bodies are burned, but I've seen no public pyre."

Time seemed to slow around Oda as the pieces began to come together. The only time Clan Beran publicly observed funeral rites was when one of its leaders or a revered member of the clan died. Most of the time, families gathered in private and didn't linger with the bodies of their loved ones.

"Death rites are not of high importance here," Oda said. "Bodies are burned in the northernmost chamber, in the crematory."

The crematory fires helped to warm the water that flowed into Fortress Halgeir's irrigation system—the very one Oda's father had helped to create. Ashes of the dead were mingled with the soil that fed the hanging gardens. In these ways, the clanspeople continued their contribution to the fortress long after death.

"So a criminal who died of plague," Iva ventured, tilting her head, "would receive no public ceremony?"

"He would not," Oda answered.

Edmund and Iva exchanged a glance, and she nodded once. "Very well. Here is what we'll say.

"After the selection, I had my men visit the dungeon to

question Jund. Since Artur suspects your sister of treason, I wanted to see what more we could learn. When they arrived at his cell, they found his body.

"We sought out a healer to inspect him—*you*, Oda, since you're also Beravakt. When you opened Jund's cell, you found signs of plague."

"And I ordered Edmun and Wren to take the body for immediate cremation, as fortress protocol dictates," Oda added, feeling a bit nauseous as she said the words. "Everyone knows the rule."

"What of those who are exposed?" Iva asked.

"If they're fit to travel, they are to cover their mouths and noses in black cloth and leave the fortress with no pretense," Oda answered, eyeing the two sentries as their faces lit with recognition. "They may return if they make a full recovery, but no sooner."

Iva tilted her head. "And the immune?"

"We can stay, as long as we complete a cleansing ritual," Oda said.

"Tell me, Oda." Iva folded her arms on the table, studying her carefully. "Is Artur immune?"

"No," Oda admitted with a sigh. "He's not."

"Then it's settled." She turned to her men. "Edmun, Wren—it has been an honor. I'll need you to start the journey back to Iathium tonight. Gather your things and leave the fortress as Oda instructed. Move with urgency; speak to no one.

"When you arrive, take word to the Rí that Stev and Gwyn remain in my charge, unexposed and unharmed."

"Of course," Edmun said, his expression grim. He and Wren rose, each offering a small bow. "The honor has been ours."

Iva reached across the table and grasped Oda's hand. "This is how we save you and your sister. Don't be afraid."

Oda wished she could believe it.

CHAPTER 23

THORNE

Thorne crept from the arena long before Oda, Iva, and the sentries began to emerge. He felt too calm, given what little information he'd just overheard. It was clear Jund had escaped the dungeon, and he had a nagging suspicion that Oda had something to do with it.

She *had* tried to leave today—and she'd all but told him that she had done something unforgivable.

He would have liked to question her in the arena, but they had all lingered for too long. Night had given way to the early hours of the morning, and he worried they might be discovered.

Rather than staying nearby, he made his rounds through the courtyard and the Arthmael's Hall, peering in to see who remained.

The hall was mostly empty, and the fortress was silent. Several men, including his Beravakt, had passed out across the tables and benches in the hall after dinner, not bothering to rise and return to their own chambers. He curled his lip in disgust, then turned back toward the courtyard.

Thorne could go to his upstairs chamber, but he would be too restless to sleep. Tomorrow, he would face Tyr in the arena and the trials would end. If he won, the marriage rite would take place.

And he would go along with every step, because he was strong enough to do his duty.

"*A strong, dutiful warrior will win respect,*" his mother had once told him. "*Without strength, he deserves nothing. He is nothing.*"

The words she'd said next had lanced his heart, and yet they had also managed to lodge themselves there. He had tried and failed to shake them off, to no avail. Now, he followed them, raging against his own better judgment in the hopes that her voice might finally be silenced.

"*Be strong, Thorne. Do not be like your father.*"

Ylanna had shamed Thorne for his admiration of Ljós, who had chosen a life of service to the people over a quest for power. She had warned Thorne that his own use of healing magic was a vulnerability. For all her talk of strength, she could only recognize it when a blade or a throne was involved.

But true strength lay in truth. In honesty. In peace. In one's ability to perceive what was wrong in the world around them and fight to correct it.

Strength was having the discernment to understand when a leader, a tradition, or a culture was misguided. It was silence where silence was appropriate, and battle when battle was necessary. And strength meant possessing the self-control to enact change in ways that did as little harm as possible.

Perhaps strength also meant walking away from intolerable circumstances, as his father had. As Oda had tried to do.

Suddenly, Thorne longed for his father. To be as close to his presence as possible. He veered from his path in the courtyard and strode toward Ljós's chambers, desperate for some sense of solace in the midst of this impossible situation.

When he arrived, he lit a torch and sat beside the pit of

stones in the center of the room, casting an orb of golden magic to illuminate them, too. Drawing a deep breath, he savored the scent of oregano, calendula, and sage, mingled with the plant essences his father had used to treat and cure so many illnesses throughout his lifetime.

From his scabbard, he drew the stone Oda had given him and held it against his heart as he stared into the soft glow of the stones.

Thorne still needed to win these trials; that fact had not changed. Letting Clan Beran fall into Tyr's hands wasn't a fate he was willing to impose on his people. But he also couldn't reconcile the idea of dutifully marrying Cynda while his love for Oda remained.

Because that was what he felt for her: love, both unconditional and forever binding. He might never be with her, but he would honor what he knew to be true.

As he watched the stones in heavy silence, he understood what he needed to do.

Rising, he crossed the room to the vast collection of herbs and supplies his father had left behind, his fingers drifting lightly over the corks as he searched.

Ljós always prepared plenty of tinctures and remedies for the healers to use as needed. They were organized in small bottles and jars of blue glass, spread across the large worktable that sat against the wall. Above it, his father had hung bundles of herbs, which had long since dried.

Thorne noted the low supply of honey, which the clanspeople routinely used for many ailments. Perhaps he should take charge of stocking the remedy ingredients now that his father was often away. That would be one way to show gratitude for Ljós's service to Clan Beran, and to continue building upon his work.

He studied the remedies until he found what he was

looking for: *sjepdraught*, which Ljós kept tucked away in a small medicine case.

Thorne took two vials from the case and closed it again, then put out the chamber lights. This wasn't the perfect answer, but it gave him the most peace, and that would have to be enough.

CHAPTER 24

ODA

When Oda arrived back at her chamber in the wee hours of the morning, Cynda sent her away. She couldn't blame her sister; after all, their plan had failed and Jund was gone. It had not been helpful to remind Cynda that at least he was still alive, because now, there was the matter of Thorne.

So Oda stepped back out into the night, leaving her sister alone in their chamber and stepping over to the railing that overlooked the courtyard.

Movement below caught her eye, and she spied Thorne crossing the courtyard and moving up the stone pathway that wound 'round the fortress. Her breath caught as she watched him trudge up and around the fortress's levels until he disappeared.

With a deep breath, she drummed her fingertips on the stone railing and began to count down the time.

Five minutes passed before she swept the area, then began to move. It would take her another ten minutes to travel from her chamber to his.

Whether or not the plan she'd concocted with Iva was

successful over the next few days, she owed Thorne an explanation.

When she arrived at his door, she gave it a light tap, then leaned against the corridor wall, carefully scanning her surroundings. Thorne didn't answer, so she tapped again. After a moment, the door cracked open, and she was met with a pair of warm amber eyes.

"You should be asleep," he said softly.

"That goes for both of us." Oda crossed her arms, shivering. "Cynda wanted me out, so I'm out."

Thorne visibly sagged, then shook his head, opening his door further. "Inside."

Oda slipped into his chamber, her cheeks heating as she attempted to ignore his bare torso. She hadn't thought this through; of course, he would be preparing to rest. Of course, he slept without a tunic.

Of course. She took a shaky breath.

He cast the silencing spell, then invited Oda to sit on his bed. Thorne took the stool across from her as she settled in, pulling one of his furs over herself. His familiar cedar-and-sage scent enveloped her, and she fought against pressing the fur to her face to savor it.

"Tell me what's happened," he said, propping an elbow on his knee and resting his chin in his hand. "I know Jund escaped. I want to hear the rest from you."

"The fewer details you know, the safer," Oda hedged. "I don't want you implicated."

He sighed. "Then tell me what to expect so the lie doesn't surprise me."

"In the morning, you'll hear talk of River Plague," she said carefully, watching his expression to gauge his reaction. "You'll hear that two of Iva's sentries were exposed, and that I authorized them to take the body for cremation."

Thorne nodded. "Good. That's protocol."

Oda relaxed a bit, though she felt puzzled by his easy acceptance. "The sentries left the fortress immediately after, to prevent the spread. Since Iva and I are immune, we're still fit to serve."

"When will Artur be told?" he asked.

"In the morning, when he comes to," she said. "He let Tyr drink him under the table tonight."

With a snort, Thorne replied, "I couldn't watch."

They shared an uneasy laugh. He ran a hand over his beard, thinking. Finally, he pressed his palms against his knees and said, "I should report to him—take you with me. It might be more convincing. And if we catch him off his guard from drink, he may not ask so many questions."

Oda drew back, tilting her head curiously. "True. When, do you think?"

"Before the Beravakt make morning rounds," he said. "I'm sure they'll be late today. But someone will notice when they feed the prisoners."

"I can do rounds. I remember the routine well enough."

"Then get to it early, and let the trainees know what you're doing." He smiled, and Oda was surprised to see his eyes light up with fondness as he watched her. "I remember it, too. I put you on dungeon duty to test your worth."

She snorted. "For a *year*. I must be worth quite a lot."

Thorne's expression softened. "You are."

He rose from the stool and joined her on the bed, sitting at the edge of the mattress. Facing her fully, he lay an upturned palm between them.

"Oda," he murmured as she stared at his hand, aching to take it, "you are worth everything."

The pain in his voice compelled her to meet his gaze. To trace his palm with her fingertips. To silence her roaring thoughts about today and all the places these final hours together shouldn't go.

There was no use reminding Thorne of what loomed ahead of them. Perhaps for the next little while, they should focus on the moment instead.

So in a tender voice, Oda said, "Last night..."

He nodded, swallowing hard. "Yes?"

Oda smiled, finally letting her gaze roam over his bare skin. The golden light of his lantern illuminated his perfectly sculpted muscles like the healing magic they shared. She hadn't let herself enjoy this sight enough that night in the bath, and she'd dearly regretted it ever since.

"It was so dark." Oda brushed her fingers over his cheek, and he exhaled, drawing a sharp, startled breath behind it. "I'd like to kiss you where I can see you—just once, while I have the chance."

Thorne moved nearer, his gaze already falling to her mouth. "Is that wise?"

She swallowed, pushing the fur aside to meet him halfway.

"No," she said as their lips met.

The kiss ignited a searing urgency that obliterated any lingering hesitation. Oda pressed a hand over his heart, drinking in his warmth as she plunged her fingertips into his hair. He'd worn it loose today, not bothering with braids or ornaments.

They clung to one another, desperate to plunder what little time they had left. Thorne slid one hand around to the small of her back, working it beneath the hem of her linen tunic. She shuddered at the tenderness in his touch, something she had not been able to experience that night in Iva's chamber.

"I want more of you, all of you," Thorne admitted, his voice low and warm. "I can't carry this secret any longer; it's too heavy."

"Let me help you bear it," Oda said, resting her palms on his chest as his fingers drifted to the laces at her collar. He pressed a kiss to her jaw as he gave them a gentle tug.

"In a little while," Thorne answered, helping her work her tunic over her head. He exhaled shakily as he cast it aside, his eyes drifting over her skin. "Right now, I am weak."

He traced her chin with his thumb as they explored one another, eyes open and searching. Piece by piece, they unraveled each other, taking their time, though there was so little of it. Oda didn't want to miss a moment, however brief, because he would never be hers again after this.

Soon, the sun would rise, and not long after that, a sleepless Thorne would face Tyr in the arena.

Oda fleetingly wondered whether she should put a stop to this and let him rest, but the feel of his lips on her skin and the reverence of his touch chased those questions away.

If this was what weakness felt like—intoxicating and wholly consuming—she may never be strong again.

They had both spent their lives proving their strength to others, and trying to convince themselves it was real in the process. In secret, they had held one another up, pushed one another to be better, each encouraging the other to grow. Perhaps, through all those moments, they had forged themselves into an unbreakable blade.

They needed one another, and if nothing else, the disasters of the past few days had finally driven them to honesty.

CHAPTER 25

THORNE

As dawn broke, Thorne cradled Oda's sleeping form in his arms. Her warm skin was a balm to his aching heart, and even after everything they'd just shared, he couldn't get close enough to her.

This would never be enough. And it pained him.

In mere hours, his entire world had changed. Thorne had changed. There was no going back to the version of himself who knew nothing of love, who'd had no desire to be vulnerable with another.

He would never be able to forget what Oda had made him feel, nor be able to erase the new image of her now emblazoned in his mind.

Oda had only been dozing for a few minutes when the grief swept him under. Now, he clung to her like a lifeline, desperate to return to the peace and certainty he'd felt when they'd finally given in.

He couldn't let her go, yet he must find a way. Their future depended on it.

Soon, these moments would become but a memory, so he would make it as clear and sharp as he could.

He shifted enough to kiss her forehead, and her grip around his body tightened as her dark lashes fluttered open. There was a brief flash of surprise in her expression, as though she had momentarily forgotten where she was. But then she smiled, brushing a strand of hair from his face.

"Did you sleep?" she asked, coaxing him down to kiss her lips.

Thorne hummed against her mouth. "How could I?"

"How could *I*?" She laughed softly. "I didn't intend to."

"You weren't out for long." He stroked her back lazily, his fingertips exploring her soft skin. "We should report to Artur soon. Tell him about the plague."

"Soon," Oda hedged, hooking a leg around him and pulling him closer. "But I've been thinking—there's something more you should know."

"You said the fewer details, the better," he reminded her, though his heart sank.

"This is critical," she said, tugging him flush against her skin. "It's something you might learn as heir, but I can't be certain."

Thorne listened as Oda recounted the story about her father and Artur in a hush. The two had forged an agreement long ago; Uden had traded Clan Énna's fire powder to Artur in exchange for the overlord's lenience.

With mounting horror, Thorne listened, wondering why he'd never questioned the contents of those barrels. They were supposed to be stockpiles of grain, dried meats, and seed for the gardens in case the clan ever had need. Now, he wondered whether they had ever truly set aside the proper stores of food.

Jund would have learned the truth, because Jund had charge over the gardens. He must have discovered the powder by accident. But telling the people would have put them at risk, so he'd directed his anger toward Iva's presence instead.

"I fear a siege," Oda whispered, "and all signs point to it."

Perhaps Jund had also harbored these fears, but he'd impulsively chosen to rebel rather than quietly devising a solution. The path Jund had chosen was an unforgivable one in the clan's eyes, but Thorne was grateful that Oda had been willing to risk herself to keep him alive.

"We'll need to locate him when this is over," Thorne said, brushing a hand over her skin. "He should know that I understand his actions."

"Yes," Oda replied, "and I'll do my best to learn where Artur sends my sister after the rite. Perhaps they can reunite."

"It would be for the best." He closed his eyes, kissing her again. "Now, there's something *you* should know."

Oda smiled sadly. "What is it?"

"This..." Thorne pressed a palm to her heart. "What has happened here cannot happen with your sister. It *will* not. There is only you."

The look in her eyes held a hundred arguments to the contrary, and a thousand admonitions to refrain from making promises he couldn't keep. She could have protested, but she didn't. He was grateful when, instead, she pushed him onto his back and silenced him with a kiss.

THEY FOUND their pleasure once more before reluctantly rising for the day. Thorne moved slowly through the painstaking steps of dressing for combat, binding his hands and donning his battle leathers with Oda's help. When he finished getting dressed, she ordered him to sit on the stool by the bed.

Gently, she combed his hair, untangling the mess she'd made of it this morning. Separating sections on the left side of his head, she began to braid.

"What weapons will you rely on in the arena?" she asked

softly, threading her fingertips gently through his long strands as she wove.

"The ones I know best," Thorne said, "and my own rage. I'll need that anger to carry out my duties."

"I hear this match is not meant to be fair. Who knows what Tyr will do?"

When she finished braiding his hair, Oda stepped in front of the stool. He tilted his face up to study her.

"I wish to stop time," Thorne said softly. "I want to be here with you, always."

"You will always have me," Oda said, bending down to kiss him. "This time, I won't break my promise."

THORNE LEFT HIS CHAMBER ALONE, heading toward the Arthmael's Hall for the morning meal. If he had calculated correctly, Oda should have plenty of time to change in her own rooms, then take over dungeon rounds before meeting him in the courtyard. Then, they would report to Artur together.

But the fortress was eerily quiet as he walked, and when he arrived at the hall, it was empty, save for a handful of ale-maidens and the families who were tasked with meal preparation this week. They had prepared bowls of porridge, arranging them in rows on the long dining tables.

"General Thorne," a middle-aged woman with silver hair and striking blue eyes addressed him softly, stepping toward him and pressing a warm bowl into his hands. She moved backward quickly, leaving a wide berth between them. "You've heard there's plague?"

"I have," Thorne answered carefully. Iva must have given word to Artur already.

"Everyone has been ordered to remain in their chambers, save for those of us who are preparing meals. The overlord says the people aren't to watch the battle today, and there will be no feast in the hall tonight."

"That's best." Thorne took a bite of porridge, trying to envision a fight with no audience. He had to fight back a grin; Tyr wouldn't be happy without a crowd to work. "A large crowd will lead to more illness."

"Begging your pardon, but there's talk that the Mór woman brought it here." A shadow crossed the woman's features. "I wouldn't be surprised."

"My father says illnesses sometimes emerge on their own," Thorne countered between bites. He accepted a cup of fresh water from one of the ale-maidens, who had drifted nearer to listen. "There's no need to cast blame. Iva Mór has a good heart, and that's what we need beside the throne."

"Your father also has a good heart," the woman said softly, her light blue eyes filling with tears. "He saved my son last year."

Thorne lowered his empty bowl, holding her gaze. He had seen her in the fortress countless times, yet he couldn't remember her name. It humbled him to realize that he knew few of his fellow clanspeople, despite his leadership role among the Beravakt.

Today, that was going to change.

"I'm glad to hear it," he said. "What is your name?"

"Mynta, General. And my son is called Bard; he wishes to join your ranks next spring." She pressed her hand to her heart and bowed her head. "I said your father has a good heart, but so do you. You have *his* heart. So good luck today; our people need you."

CHAPTER 26

ODA

Oda bathed hastily in her chamber, changing into clean clothes and arming herself like usual.

She was tempted to give in to guilt for spending the morning in Thorne's bed, but she wouldn't allow her memories of that time to be ruined. They were the only ones she would have, so she would do her best to preserve them, untarnished by regret or thoughts of what might have been.

Oda pulled on her soft leather boots and tied her hair back at her nape. Then, she stepped back out into the morning sun.

When she opened the door, Gwyn—one of Iva's sentries—was standing there, fist raised, as though she'd been preparing to knock. The slight, red-haired guard started, then took a step back and gave a little bow.

"My lady has sent for you," she said. Her voice was almost too soft and gentle to belong to a soldier. "She says I'm not to fear, that you've already had River Plague. Is that true?"

"Yes, it is," Oda said, stepping out and shutting the door behind her. "I had it as a child."

Gwyn exhaled shakily. "Good. Because I never have. It was

eerie to walk the corridors alone, so the journey back will be better."

Oda's heart drummed as she and Gwyn started down the long, spiraling stone pathway toward the courtyard. Gwyn had been right; there was almost no one about the fortress, and the silence was unfamiliar. If Artur had heard the news, then she had no need to make rounds in the dungeon, after all.

She wasn't sure whether to feel relieved or worried about that revelation.

"What do they do in Iathium when there's illness?" Oda asked.

"Well, I live in the barracks," said Gwyn, "so when someone there gets ill, the general sends everyone home until it passes. If it extends to the Dome, then the courtiers go home, as well. But out in the city, most everyone has their own homes, so sick households keep to themselves."

Oda's brows scrunched. "And your healers?"

"They mostly make medicines from plants," said Gwyn. "Like yours."

Oda suppressed a smile. She wasn't sure how long it would be before Iva's sentries observed Clan Beran's healing magic for themselves, or if they ever would. But it was clear this young soldier had not witnessed magic yet.

All the way to Iva's chambers, Oda kept Gwyn talking, asking questions about the city and her life there.

As they walked, she carefully observed what was happening around them and who was moving about the fortress. When they finally arrived at Iva's chamber, Gwyn left Oda there and excused herself to the room next door.

When Iva opened the chamber door, Oda sucked in a breath; the overlord's intended looked like magic personified. She donned a flowing gown of gold, with small white flowers woven into her long, dark curls. Her lips were stained with a dark, glossy pink, and she'd dusted a light layer of golden powder across the apples of her cheeks.

"Come in," she urged, beckoning Oda to enter. "We don't have much time."

"I take it Artur was already notified?" Oda asked, slipping inside.

"Overnight," said Iva, motioning for her to sit after closing the door. "The night watch spotted my sentries leaving with their face-coverings."

They took opposite ends of the bench that sat at the foot of Iva's bed, facing one another.

"What I wouldn't give to have my own measure of healing magic right about now," Iva whispered. "The terror transformed Artur. I could scarcely calm him."

"How awful," Oda replied.

"How *effective*. Artur wanted to cancel the match between Thorne and Tyr today, but I convinced him to let it go forward. We must take advantage of the state he's in."

Oda pressed her fingers to her mouth, leaning forward in spite of herself. "Berav, help him."

"But not too soon." Iva grinned conspiratorially. "So the battle will go on, but there will be no audience. He's too afraid disease will spread. Everyone without immunity must remain in their chambers for three days until we're sure no one else has fallen ill."

"I see," Oda said. Dread coiled low in her belly, and she fought down the surge of disappointment. She had hoped to be there for Thorne. "I assume the marriage rite will go forward, as well."

"It will."

Oda tried to ignore the sinking feeling, but it was impossible. "Where's my sister?"

"I can take you to her," Iva said. "That's why I sent for you. This is the only chance you'll have to say a proper goodbye."

"Can you find out where Artur will send her?" Oda asked, grasping Iva's hands.

"I'll try, but I can't promise you anything."

They emerged into the empty corridor again, and Iva held Oda's hand, leading her toward a pathway that would take them to the fortress's upper levels.

Down this corridor, all the torches had been put out, so that they moved in complete darkness. Up and up, they went, winding through the hallways and moving into the building's interior, toward an uppermost row of stone chambers.

"This is where the girls are being kept," Iva whispered. "Their doors are locked from the outside. Go to the room on the far end of the corridor—the very end, in the center. Under no circumstances are you to leave the way we came.

"There is a hidden passageway behind a tapestry on the eastern wall. When you're ready to go, it will take you back to an outlet on the second level—near the gardens, I believe."

"Thank you," Oda breathed, squeezing her hand.

"Move quickly," Iva said. "I'll bring Cynda to you."

As quickly as she dared, Oda fumbled her way down the dark corridor. Candlelight emanated dimly from beneath each door, giving her enough illumination to spot the chamber Iva had mentioned. When she reached it, she lifted the latch as slowly and quietly as she could, then let herself inside.

The rich beauty of the spacious chamber drew a sharp gasp from her. It was a room she might have imagined in Iathium's Dome, worlds apart from Clan Beran's minimal, yet comfortable, trappings. There was color in every conceivable space—even on the bed, which was spread with a rainbow of dyed silks and linens of red, gold, and orange.

This chamber's position on Fortress Halgeir's uppermost floor gave it the advantage of sunlight, which streamed in through a skylight covered by crystal-clear glass. A large fire roared in the hearth on the north side of the room, and there,

Oda spotted the tapestry Iva had mentioned. Its decorative stitching depicted Clan Beran's beautiful hanging gardens, populated by gardeners and warriors from a different time.

Colorful tapestries and banners hung on every wall of the room, and Oda took her time walking its perimeter, studying the art with curiosity.

The most attractive pieces in the fortress that she'd been aware of were the large wooden doors outside the Arthmael's Hall. So much of the woodwork found around the fortress was beautifully crafted, but Clan Beran's people were otherwise not given to artistic endeavors.

Instead, the people of this clan were offered two options for their life pursuits: utility or combat. Woodworking was useful, but weaving and painting and sculpting were not, according to the overlord and the clan's elders.

The door snicked open again, and instinctively, Oda moved aside, pressing herself against the wall. A moment later, Iva swept in wearing her gold gown, and Cynda followed.

Oda pressed a hand to her mouth at the sight of her sister. Cynda was resplendent in a gown of shimmering violet, the color their father's magic might have been. She wore a gold circlet atop her black hair, which had been arranged into small braids, then pinned back to hold the circlet in place. Her skin was more beautiful than ever in the warm firelight.

If Oda hadn't known better, she might have thought Cynda a queen.

"Oda," Iva called softly.

Her sister whirled when she stepped away from the wall. Relief relaxed her features, and she held out her arms to Oda, who rushed into her embrace. The girls clutched one another tightly, and Oda's eyes stung with tears.

"I shouldn't have sent you away last night," Cynda whispered. "When you never came back, I feared for you."

"You needed the space," Oda replied. "I'm fine, you see?"

Cynda pulled back and gripped her sister's shoulders. "And *I* will be fine. I'm just glad Jund is alive."

"Perhaps one day, there will be a way to right this," Oda said with a sigh. "Thorne is a good man—" the words caught in her throat, and she had to fight the urge to weep. "And you'll have nothing to fear from him. He'll be good to you."

"And what if Tyr defeats Thorne?" Cynda asked grimly. "Can you say the same of him?"

"Thorne *must* win," Iva said, stepping in to lay a hand on Cynda's shoulder. "There's simply no other choice."

Oda hadn't given herself time to think of what might occur if Tyr did win, and she couldn't afford to now. There was no ideal outcome to any of this; at least if Thorne married her sister, she would know there was nothing to fear.

As much as she tried to convince herself that simple reassurance would be enough to move forward, she knew it would not.

Without the joy and peace she'd experienced in Thorne's arms this morning, Oda's future felt empty and vast. She and Cynda had once ached to belong here, yet look where that had gotten them. This belonging would be meaningless without Thorne, and for the first time, Oda truly wished she had never set foot in Fortress Halgeir.

CHAPTER 27

THORNE

Facing Tyr in the arena was nothing like Thorne had envisioned.

They took their places in the center of the arena floor, overseen by Artur and Iva, who sat together in their own box high above.

Admittedly, Thorne had anticipated the energy of a roaring crowd—likely just as much as Tyr had. When it came time to face one another in the empty arena's vast expanse, engulfed by stark quiet, he couldn't help but feel stripped of any bravado he might have had otherwise.

"I'll go easy to start," Tyr said, adjusting the wraps that covered his knuckles. "You might be shocked at how many new fighting skills you can learn outside this fortress."

Thorne said nothing, but rolled his shoulders and inhaled deeply. Holding eye contact without a word was the fastest way to silence a talker; he knew this from his many years of experience in this arena.

No matter what Tyr claimed, the mere fact that he'd needed to say it aloud told Thorne everything about his opponent's mindset.

He drew his broadsword and shield, sinking into a fighting stance. Tyr drew his own blade in kind, raising his own shield and assuming an unfamiliar stance that looked more like a flourish than anything useful. Thorne refrained from rolling his eyes, as Oda would if she were watching.

The thought of her brought memories of this morning rushing in.

But uncontrolled, these thoughts would put him at risk, especially here. He counted his breaths, willed the visions away, and dragged his focus back to his opponent.

Long ago, Artur had trained Thorne to fight on this very floor. He recalled a lesson the overlord had taught him as a boy, about finding a focal point on which to set his attention. Thorne scanned Tyr, looking for that point until he found it: a small satchel that hung around Tyr's neck at the end of a long cord.

It was foolish to wear trinkets of any kind into the ring, but then again, Tyr was quite stupid. So Thorne would let it pass, and he would focus on that emblem of idiocy until the fight was done.

"Who you thinking about, hmm?" Tyr adjusted his grip as he leaned in a bit, a sneer curling his lips suggestively. "That little warrior you favor?"

Thorne flicked his gaze up to where Artur and Iva sat. The overlord had not yet risen, so Thorne remained silent.

"I know what you feel for her," Tyr continued. "But if you win today, you'll marry the overlord's choice. If I win, you die. Either way, she will not be yours."

She's already mine, Thorne wanted to say.

The rage he had invoked earlier now blazed to new heights. It heated in his belly, spreading outward through his torso, up his throat, down his limbs. His best strategy was to keep it under control, then unleash when the moment was right.

"I don't intend to die," Thorne said, "and I won't end you. But if you continue to speak, I might change my mind."

Tyr smirked. "You will never best me. Wait 'til you see why."

Movement caught his eye as Artur stepped to the edge of the box, resting his palms on the stone railing.

"Begin." His booming voice echoed around the empty room until it fell, lackluster, into nothingness.

Tyr raised a brow, as though they were exchanging a private joke. Under any other circumstances, this ridiculous display might have been amusing.

Thorne raised his sword for the first strike, and they moved into rhythmic combat. To his surprise, Tyr could hold up with some of his better fighters. Tyr's stamina was comparable to the younger warriors, like Mjit and Rynd—perhaps a bit hardier. It was enough to keep Thorne, who had not slept for the past two nights, on his toes.

On a regular day, Thorne might have quickly squashed Tyr. But he wanted to treat this as more of a show of control than a display of wild, untethered brutishness. Any warrior of Thorne's caliber could pummel an opponent in a few strikes and be done with it. For him, this was about proving his value as a leader.

And as a leader, brute strength could never be Thorne's first line of defense.

It was quickly apparent that Tyr's sword skill was no match for Thorne's—even with the odd, unfamiliar technique thrown in.

Clearly, Tyr had picked up some of the sentries' moves in Iathium, as well as a few more unfamiliar moves along the way. But he wasn't the swordsman he thought he was.

Thorne pushed Tyr to his limits, striking and blocking until the former's stamina began to wane.

It took steady persistence to begin breaking him down, but the signs were beginning to show. He noted that Tyr was no longer able to lift his sword as high as before and that his lean, muscular arms had begun to tremble with the effort of it.

There was a commotion from behind Tyr, and Thorne glanced up to see his Beravakt filing into the arena, lining up in the lowest seats opposite of Artur's box. They were over one hundred fifty in number; though the empty vastness of the arena engulfed them, their arrival filled Thorne with resolve. He took a breath, reinvigorated despite Artur's enraged expression.

They would likely be punished for defying Artur's orders to stay away. Still, it seemed that the overlord intended for this fight to move forward regardless.

Thorne fixated on his focal point again, then met Tyr's eyes. He opened his mouth to speak, but Thorne moved quickly, forcing him on the defensive instead.

They clashed with renewed vigor. Thorne had not seen Oda among the Beravakt, but he forced the thought from his mind. He couldn't afford to become distracted right now.

He had to win.

For all of them.

From the seats, a low, steady drumming began. The Beravakt had brought their spears, and they beat them against the floor in time, chanting his name in low tones.

Thorne. Thorne. Thorne.

Tyr surged forward, putting Thorne on the defensive this time. He blocked several hard strikes, sidestepping Tyr's lunge as he attempted to drive his blade home. That move sent Tyr stumbling forward, and for the first time, his opponent lost his footing.

A great cheer rose from the crowd that had gathered in the arena. For the first time, an astonished Thorne realized that the *clan*—not just his warriors—had openly defied Artur's decree. Hundreds of people filled the seats now, and more were pouring in from the main entrance. They chanted and drummed along with the Beravakt, and a rush of renewed energy swept through Thorne.

Suddenly, he felt more alert and alive. That was *his* name on the people's lips. He thought of the woman who had served him breakfast this morning, and her words rang through his mind once again.

"Our people need you."

Contempt flashed across Tyr's features. His lip curled into a sneer, and his gaze hardened.

"Look at their blind devotion," he said.

"You're beginning to sound winded," Thorne replied coolly, emboldened by the gathering crowd. "Perhaps you should stop your goading, catch your breath."

Tyr laughed, wild-eyed as he swung his blade in a wide arc. "And who was breathless this morning, under cover of darkness? Or did you think no one would notice her slip into your chamber?"

The din in the arena was loud enough to swallow Tyr's words, but Thorne could hear them, and that was all it took to make him stumble.

Tyr lunged into the follow-through, slashing upward. The tip of his blade barely skimmed Thorne's torso, but it was enough to slash his clothing and draw blood. He ground his teeth against the sting, grateful it was only a shallow wound.

Howling with laughter, Tyr raised his arms to work the crowd. But rather than shouting his name, they jeered and hissed.

From above, Artur was leering down at Thorne, the disappointment clear in his expression.

Thorne adjusted his shield, preparing to meet his opponent's next blow. This time, Tyr struck clumsily from his side, bringing his blade around as though to slash at Thorne's ribs. But Thorne caught his blade on the edge of his shield, where it lodged and stuck. He ripped the sword out of Tyr's grip, throwing his shield across the arena with it.

The weapons clattered hard against the stone wall, and Tyr was left with only a shield in hand. His dark eyes went wide, his mirth melting away.

Thorne advanced on him, drawing his axe with his right hand and brandishing his sword in his left.

And Tyr turned and ran from him, letting his shield clatter to the floor.

The roaring crowd grew louder. So loud that Thorne could feel their drumming in his bones.

Victory swelled in Thorne's chest, but the fight wasn't over. Too little blood had been spilled, and he knew this outcome wouldn't satisfy Artur. Thorne wouldn't be considered a true victor if he simply allowed his opponent to retreat.

He would need to prevail—visibly and without question.

So he broke into a run, chasing Tyr in the direction of the fallen weapons. Thorne quickly discovered that swiftness was Tyr's greatest talent in combat, because his opponent reached the arena wall in moments. Tyr wrenched a torch from its sconce and moved back toward the center of the arena, not bothering to retrieve his sword.

Thorne halted and turned to face Tyr, readying his weapons again. "Pick up your blade," he growled, advancing.

Tyr grinned, an uneasy laugh breaking from him. "I don't need blades, Thorne Beran. And yours are no use." He pointed the torch at Thorne for emphasis. "This is a new era for Clan Beran. Our people needn't live like peasants when we could have all the riches of Rodhlan at our feet."

Focal point. Thorne refocused on the satchel around Tyr's neck, just as his opponent reached up to brush it with his fingertips.

In that exact moment, he'd said, *riches of Rodhlan.*

Suddenly, Tyr's boast from last night's feast echoed in Thorne's mind.

Let us say the overlord harbors secrets that strengthen us in... unnatural ways. And let us say that he believes himself the sole custodian of those secrets.

Tyr's fingers closed around the satchel, and the world around Thorne slowed.

He calculated the distance between himself and Tyr. There wouldn't be much time to act. Tyr had all he needed in his grasp already: fire powder and a torch to ignite it.

Thorne's one advantage was that Tyr had no idea how much he knew.

"You're stalling," Thorne shouted. "Come meet me with your blade. I'll give you more time to pick it up, unless you want to run away again."

In his periphery, he could see Artur move to the box's railing, peering down to get a better look.

"Everyone but *her*, it seems," Tyr said, his eyes wild.

He lunged in Thorne's direction, thrusting the torch like he would a sword. The bag swung precariously on its cord, and Thorne moved back to preserve the wide berth between them.

Tyr hissed, "Where is she, Thorne? Waiting in your bed? When I get to your chamber, I'll be sure to tell her how you died."

Gritting his teeth, Tyr wrenched the cord from around his neck. Thorne couldn't wait any longer; he had to act. In a split second, he made his decision.

Taking several running strides backward, Thorne threw his axe. It sailed end over end, finding its mark in Tyr's forehead. Tyr crumpled to his knees, then fell on his torch.

And the entire arena went bright white.

CHAPTER 28

ODA

"What was that?"

Oda froze in her seat by the fire, listening intently. Cynda's brow creased with concern, and she strained to hear, too. There was a low rumbling that sounded distant, yet loose stones and fine dust began to tumble from the walls around them.

"Is the ground quaking?" Cynda asked.

"No, it's quiet now," Oda said. "Listen."

They sat in silence a few moments longer. Sure enough, they heard nothing else.

A ground-quake usually meant sustained rumbling and shaking. It was something the people of Fortress Halgeir dreaded, since they lived in a structure built entirely of upthrust stone. History had it that the massive, jutting rock had, itself, been formed by a quake, so the clanspeople were forever on alert for signs of unusual movement.

This noise—this impact—had only happened once, and now it seemed to be over. But something wasn't right, and a nagging sense of unease settled deep in her chest.

"Where did it come from?" Cynda's voice was low.

"I..."

Oda tried to picture where their current chamber was positioned. Her heart sank as she realized it must be somewhere above the arena. A wave of fear washed over her, tightening her throat.

This match was not to be a fair fight; she'd known that much before she and Thorne had parted. Whatever was happening down there, whatever they had heard, it was unnatural.

And suddenly, she realized just how inadequate her goodbye to Thorne had been this morning.

Oda had taken it for granted that he would survive this day. She'd expected to remain his trusted warrior and confidante. And she had let him walk away from his chamber *knowing* that she would see him again after this battle.

But what if she had been wrong?

What if Tyr *had* found an unfair advantage in the fire powder Jund had warned her about?

She grasped her sister's hand, pressing a shaking hand to her mouth.

"Oda, what is it?" Cynda demanded, squeezing Oda's hand. "What's wrong?"

"He's dead," Oda said. "He has to be."

Cynda's eyes went wide, and she shook her head. "What are you talking about?"

"It's Tyr—Tyr won the trials." Tears streamed down Oda's cheeks as the truth sank in. "He had Papa's fire powder. That's what we heard."

Cynda grasped Oda's face, tears welling in her eyes, too. "If this is true, we do not linger. We kill Tyr, and we *run*—together. Tonight. I don't care what Artur threatens to do; we know the truth about Papa. Jund told me about the weapon. Artur will stand down where our family is concerned, or we'll lay siege to this fortress ourselves. Are you with me?"

Oda nodded, though her entire body trembled. She was fully armed; making quick work of Tyr would be easy. And if he had indeed killed her Thorne tonight, then it would be a pleasure.

CHAPTER 29

THORNE

The explosion's force threw Thorne across the arena floor, slamming him hard against the stone wall. For a moment, the space had gone bright white from the intensity of the blast. Now, the atmosphere was cloaked in a smoky haze.

In the center of the arena, Tyr's body lay burnt and mangled. The smell of charred flesh made Thorne nauseous.

Thorne scanned the floor, spotting the axe he'd used to deliver the killing blow. Its smooth, carved wooden handle was now charred and burning, its blade smeared with ash.

People were clambering over one another to escape the arena. Thorne could see hundreds of them pouring up the stairs and out of the room as quickly as they could. Only his Beravakt remained, watching in stunned silence as Thorne groaned, pushing himself up onto his hands and knees.

His ears rang and his vision blurred. Still, he found his broadsword and grasped its hilt. With much effort, he rose to his feet, fighting the sudden dizziness that overtook him as he searched for Artur's hulking form in the box above.

But the box was empty, and the overlord was nowhere to be found.

How *dare* he vanish the moment Thorne prevailed? He would take his rightful place, whether Artur acknowledged his heirdom today or not. Thorne had come too far to be denied or dismissed now.

"Artur!" Thorne roared into the vast arena. "Artur Beran!"

"*Thorne.*"

He turned toward the sound of Iva's voice and found her standing near the lower entryway that led to the war room. Her expression was grim. "He's in the war room. Come."

Thorne tilted his head, confusion further clouding his thoughts. The words that rolled off her tongue were in... *Brylla.*

Iva must have sworn fealty to Artur. Beran's language was never gifted to *anyone* without that sacrifice. It was a magical transfer of knowledge that eased loyal outsiders' transition into fortress life.

She extended a hand, and Thorne stared at it numbly for a long moment. Then, he looked into her eyes. There was compassion and quiet strength there, and for the first time, he was deeply grateful Artur had brought this outsider into their midst.

"Come," Iva repeated, "so the overlord can congratulate his heir."

But when they entered the war room, Artur's expression was anything but congratulatory. He ordered Thorne to lock the door behind him, so Thorne obliged. Iva sat beside Artur, but the overlord held up a hand, calling Thorne to a halt.

"No closer," he ordered. "I fear I am falling ill."

Truly, his face looked ashen—whether from fear or true sickness, Thorne couldn't be entirely sure.

"My thanks, Lord," Thorne said. "I'm not immune to plague."

"Then we must end this quickly," Artur said, leaning forward. "How did you know what Tyr possessed?"

"Your pardon, my lord, but how did Tyr know?" Thorne countered. "He was as good as a privateer. It concerns me that this information could exist beyond these walls."

"*How*?" Artur repeated.

Thorne fought to keep his expression impassive. "Last night at the feast, he bragged that you possessed a weapon that would give Clan Beran an unnatural advantage. He claimed that our people could become wealthy from the sale of it."

He expected Artur to press him again, so he added, "Iteloria possesses such weapons. On the arena floor, Tyr said he had no need of a blade. When I saw the satchel around his neck, I acted. That's all, my lord."

Thorne hoped his lie would ring true; he had no knowledge of Itelorian weapons. When he glanced at Iva, her eyes were shining, and she gave him an almost imperceptible nod of approval.

"Then in ending Tyr, you have done Clan Beran a service," Artur said. "Knowledge of fire-powder was to be part of your inheritance, and so you've received it. There will be much to learn in the coming years."

"And what of the people, my lord?" Iva asked softly. "All those who witnessed the blast?"

"We'll tell them it came from Iteloria," Artur answered, "and nothing more."

Iva inclined her head. "Yes, my lord."

"I must retire," Artur said, pressing his fingertips to his brow. "My head aches and my sight grows dim."

"What of the marriage rite?" Iva pressed.

"You will complete it in my stead as proxy, Iva, as your first act of service to the clan," Artur answered, his voice growing weak. "Since our own binding was completed this morning, I have full trust in you to perform Thorne's. The runestone will do the work for you."

Iva bowed her head. "As you wish."

"We must have this done to protect against plague. Surely, the people's disobedience in the arena will yield many cases."

Iva and Thorne exchanged a fleeting glance. "Hopefully it won't, my lord."

"What more do you require of me?" Thorne asked.

"We'll anoint you in ceremony when the plague has passed," Artur answered, "but you've proven yourself worthy. My final requirement is your obedient marriage and your secrecy in the matter of the fire powder."

"It will be done, my lord," Thorne answered solemnly.

ARTUR LEFT Thorne and Iva alone in the war room, taking the Beravakt with him on his way out of the arena.

Iva scrutinized Thorne, wrinkling her nose. "You'll need to clean up before your binding rite. There's a bathing chamber in your suite, so there's no need to return to your own room."

Thorne looked down, noticing for the first time that he was covered in blood and soot. The slash across his chest had begun to clot, and his tunic's torn cloth was stuck to the dried blood. He extended his arms and turned his hand over, noting the grime on his skin.

"You're truly Artur's wife now?" he asked.

Iva gave him a shallow nod. "He said binding ourselves sooner rather than later would give him hope of surviving this plague. I dared not refuse. There will still be a celebration, but not for some time."

"Ah." Thorne closed his eyes and heaved a breath.

"It's a simple ceremony," Iva added. "It will be over quickly, but you must prepare."

"I need to see Oda," he said absently.

Once the words had left his mouth, he realized his mistake. He drew in a sharp breath, looking up to see Iva studying him.

"Then I'll make sure you do," Iva said. She nodded to the space behind Thorne. "Are those your things?"

He'd forgotten that he had hastily packed a change of clothing.

Thorne rose, his body aching from the arena as he bent to retrieve his satchel. As he lifted it, the vials of *sjepdraught* from his father's chamber rolled out of its open flap and across to the floor. The racket caught Iva's attention, and she rose, too, bending down to swipe them up.

"What's this?" she asked, holding them up.

"A tincture my father prepares," Thorne lied. "Aphrodisiac."

"Ah." Iva handed them back, pursing her lips. "I'm sure that won't be necessary."

Thorne tucked the vials back into his bag and slung the strap over his shoulder, trudging from the room. He stepped aside to let Iva lead, then they began their long trek toward the fortress's northernmost rooms.

As they emerged from the arena, a handful of Beravakt warriors fell in to flank them. The fortress was no longer deathly still as it had been that morning, but it was more somber. Clanspeople lined the pathway out of the arena and crowded in the courtyard to catch a glimpse of Artur's newly-appointed heir.

Most bowed their heads and placed a fist over their hearts to show respect. Some murmured his name.

He decided not to focus on any one face, for he feared meeting the contempt of those who had loved Tyr. Most of all, he did not want to lock eyes with Tyr's mother and father, nor the younger siblings he'd left behind.

Finally, to Thorne's relief, they reached a corridor shrouded in darkness. The Beravakt broke off to line the corridor's entrance, blocking spectators from following. In this way, Thorne and Iva made the rest of the trek alone and in silence.

By the time they reached the door to the wedding chamber, Thorne's heart was pounding and his stomach twisting. He tried to conjure calming magic for himself, but the small orb flickered out. In the dark, the magic's glow caught Iva's attention, and she turned to him.

"It will turn out far better than you fear," Iva said softly. "I know this to be true." She unlocked the door for Thorne, then stepped aside. "Enter. I'll follow."

Roaring filled Thorne's head and his limbs felt disconnected from his body as he stepped over the threshold. This was it; he had made it this far through the trials. Completing the marriage was his final task, and it would all be over.

He had barely advanced two steps when a familiar voice called out.

"Don't come any closer or I swear, I'll take your life."

Oda stepped into view, brandishing her axe. But when she saw Thorne standing there, her eyes went wide, and the weapon fell from her grasp, clattering to the floor. She doubled over, pressing her hands to her knees as though she might faint.

Without thinking, Thorne met her in a few long strides, grasping her forearms to help her to the floor. She sat, pulling her knees to her chest and cradling her head in her hands.

"Alive." Oda's voice was thick with emotion as she raised her head to look at him. Her eyes were puffy and bloodshot, as though she'd already been in tears for some time. "You're alive, you're alive."

Thorne knelt before Oda, skimming his palms up her arms and over her shoulders in soothing strokes. Along the way, he conjured his healing magic, working to calm her despite his own discomfort. He cupped the back of her neck, then pressed his forehead against hers.

"Hush," he soothed. "I swore I would win."

Oda returned the gesture, and the feel of her palm on his neck made him shiver. Transported him back to the memories of this morning. He released a shaky breath, chasing the thoughts away for the thousandth time.

"I should *kill* you for scaring me like that," she murmured. "What happened down there?"

"Tyr tried to use the fire powder to his advantage," Thorne answered as they reluctantly released one another. "He did not succeed."

"He's dead, then?" Cynda stepped forward, sinking to her knees beside them. Her wary eyes flicked between Oda and Thorne, as if their closeness was an entirely new revelation to her.

"Yes," Thorne said, putting a wider berth between himself and Oda. "That wasn't my intent, but I had no choice."

"You did what you had to," Cynda said softly, her gaze downcast. "Like all of us must."

The soft rustle of Iva's gown alerted them to her presence. She settled on a bench by the hearth, watching the three intently.

"I'm learning we all have parts to play," Iva began quietly, "and yet, things aren't always what they seem. Do you agree?"

Cynda's expression was solemn as she bowed her head. "Yes, my lady."

"You see, tonight I am playing a role," Iva continued.

She bent to lift a large, smooth stone from the floor by the hearth, settling it in her lap. Upon closer inspection, Thorne could see that hundreds of runes had been etched into its surface. They were runes of power, of prayer, of healing. Among them, he recognized many of the familiar letters and shapes his father had taught him in childhood.

This stone, however, was a relic Thorne had never laid eyes on.

Iva continued, "The overlord has developed signs of illness, so he has asked me to stand in for him as proxy. As his wife, I'm at liberty to do so. For all intents and purposes, I *am* Artur. Do you understand?"

Oda's jaw dropped, and she glanced at Thorne in surprise. He nodded to confirm Iva's news. "Artur begged off?"

"Plague," Iva said, lowering her voice an octave to mimic Artur's growl. "A grave threat, indeed."

Thorne grinned in spite of himself. When Oda caught his eye, she smiled, too.

"And so, I ask each of you…" Iva leaned nearer, searching each face in turn: Thorne, Oda, Cynda. "Are you willing to play the roles I assign as Artur? Your sovereign demands full obedience, just so we're clear."

Thorne studied her face. Iva, this outsider who had captured Artur's heart, wasn't what he had expected her to be. She was shrewd and intelligent, and so much more than he'd given her credit for. In those ways, she was like his Oda; the outsider-turned-warrior who had anchored herself in Thorne's soul.

For all the ways Artur had shown himself lacking as a leader, Iva had stepped in to smooth the path forward.

Despite his misgivings, Thorne found himself trusting her completely. If full obedience to Artur meant following Iva's orders in this moment, then he could bring himself to obey.

"Thorne, you know the role you've won," Iva began. "Your duty is to see it through to its full potential. Over the next five years, you'll be tasked with earning the people's loyalty. That is your primary concern: to have the support of a clan who will follow you anywhere, whatever you do."

"I understand," Thorne said.

Iva turned to Oda next. "Oda, your role as warrior and adviser to Thorne is essential. That's what you'll continue to portray to the clan. Loyalty, wisdom, strength—these are the attributes they should continue to see from you."

Oda looked crestfallen, but she kept her attention fixed on Iva, who went on to address her sister.

"Cynda," Iva continued, "As the selection process requires total secrecy on pain of death, your former role at Fortress Halgeir is complete. We have five years to determine recourse for today's events."

Cynda's brow creased with confusion. "I don't understand."

"I am Artur," Iva replied. "You needn't understand. Things aren't always what they seem."

"Yes, my lord," Oda said with a little smirk.

Iva grinned. "Below the surface, there's more, so let us dive deeper. Who's to say that an heir and his second-in-command can't be united in more than one way? Who's to say that a loyal people would be unforgiving of deeper bonds, were they to come to light in the future?"

Thorne's heart began to thunder just as Oda whipped around to gape at him, then at Iva. This couldn't be; it wasn't possible.

But then Iva said, "Artur demands an obedient marriage, Thorne Beran. If Artur were to alter his original decision, to select a match who would complement your strengths both as a ruler and as a warrior, would you obey?"

Oda reached out to clutch his hand, squeezing hard. Emotion gripped Thorne by the throat, choking his words as he answered, "I would."

Cynda sank into a seated position on the floor, covering her mouth with her hands. "Please, let this be real," she whispered to herself, though Thorne could hear every word. "Please, *please*."

"As Artur's proxy," Iva said, "I order a marriage bond between Thorne and Oda, thereby binding Uden Énna's bloodline to the overlord's throne."

CHAPTER 30
ODA

Oda had never seen Thorne shed tears before today. But when he turned to her and reached for her cheek, his eyes were shining.

She resisted the urge to lose herself in his touch, reluctantly turning to Iva instead.

"How?" she demanded. "How is this supposed to work?"

"One day at a time," Iva answered. "That's all we have."

"Artur threatened our entire family if we don't comply with his wishes," Oda said softly. "What happens when he learns the truth?"

"We remind him of what we know," Thorne answered. "You should have seen his face today when he realized I knew of the fire powder. He'll spend the foreseeable future fighting to contain the information."

"How did Tyr learn of it?" Cynda asked.

"He likely plied Artur with drink," said Iva.

It was true that Artur and Tyr had spent many recent nights drinking together in the hall. But Artur had never been known to spill Clan Beran's secrets from drink alone.

"Artur only shares secrets strategically," Oda mused. "Even drunk, he's tight-lipped when it comes to the clan."

Thorne nodded. "She's right."

Fleetingly, Oda wondered whether Artur had given Tyr the information intentionally. She thought back to Tyr's strange behavior in the dungeon, and Artur's delight at his suggestions for torture and execution. The two had seemed oddly close, and she and Thorne had surmised that Tyr offered some measure of political or diplomatic influence Artur coveted.

Oda swallowed, her sense of unease growing at the thought. "I think that's a question we'll need to answer in the near future, if we want to protect our people."

"The marriage," Cynda pressed in a soft voice. "We have to deal with that first."

Thorne and Oda exchanged a glance. His cheeks were flushed, his breathing rapid. She wanted to take his hand, but restrained herself; she still wasn't convinced Iva's proxy scheme had any merit.

"Clan Beran's leaders are known for their impeccable secrecy," Iva said. "If we can all embrace that secrecy ourselves, we should have time to determine our next moves."

"I could disappear into the wilderness," Cynda mused. "Cross the Strait. Assume a new name."

Iva shrugged. "Perhaps in time. I believe there are possibilities."

"I wanted to reunite you with Jund, Cynda," said Oda.

"Just knowing he's alive is more than I hoped for," Cynda said, smiling at her sister, "but I would give everything to find him."

Thorne kept his gaze trained on Oda as he asked, "Iva, how much time do we have tonight?"

Iva's brow creased in thought. "As much time as we can buy with that sleeping draught you've hidden in your satchel, I suppose."

Thorne paled, and Oda burst out laughing. "*Sjepdraught*? That's how you planned to avoid tonight?"

With a sheepish expression, Thorne grumbled, "I was going to dose us both, Cynda and myself, so we would *sleep*." Grudgingly, he handed his satchel to Iva.

"Aphrodisiac, indeed," Iva chuckled, rummaging through its contents to extract the vials. She snorted. "I'll take these. Artur needs some deep, restorative sleep if he's going to recover properly."

Oda laughed until tears ran down her cheeks. Cynda joined in, leaning near to place a hand on Thorne's shoulder. She gave him a little shove.

"I like you more than I thought, you brute," she laughed, breaking into a relieved smile. "You and Oda should obey proxy-Artur and put yourselves out of your misery. *Please.* Otherwise, we're about to have a very long nap together."

Thorne smiled, his attention never leaving Oda. "I'm willing to obey."

He extended his hand to Oda, and she took it, lacing her fingers through his. She wasn't sure *how* this deception could end well, but every option in their path seemed impossible in one way or another. At least this way, she would have more time with Thorne.

After all that had happened, he was truly what she wanted most.

"As am I," Oda said.

ON IVA'S ORDERS, Thorne retreated to the bathing chamber to wash away the grime of the arena. Oda, Cynda, and Iva were left alone in the main chamber, where they went to work assembling an altar for the binding rite. There was a tall, heavy stone sitting against the far wall, and they worked

together to move it to the center of the room before the
hearth.

Iva set the runestone atop it. Immediately, a number of the
runes etched into its surface began to glow a soft white. Oda
recognized symbols whose surface meanings were *devotion,
duty, loyalty,* and *respect.* In combination, they represented
something much more profound: the depth and breadth of a
love that could stand the test of time.

"Now, here are the next steps." Iva was still gazing at the
stone in wonder. "Artur must give me a secret word for the
couple. Once I have it, I'll make sure he takes his rest, lest he
decide to remove proxy and attend the rite himself."

Oda and Cynda exchanged a glance. "What would you have
us do?" Cynda asked.

"Exchange clothing," Iva said. "You and I will take the
hidden passage, Cynda, then return in the morning. Oda can
use the same pathway to get back to her chamber when it's
time."

Cynda needed no persuading. She turned her back to Iva
for help with the intricate lacing that secured the gown. Oda
began hastily stripping off layers of her own clothing and
weapons, her fingers trembling as she went.

Once they'd exchanged the base layers, Iva let herself out of
the room, promising to return within the hour. Cynda went to
work lacing the gown to fit Oda's frame.

"What will Mum say when she learns what's happened?"
she mused.

"I don't want to think about it," Oda answered. "But remember, all she needs to know is that you were among the elect."

"Five years is a long time to go without her," Cynda said
quietly, coming around to face Oda. She grasped Oda's hands.
"And without you."

"What's happened here isn't right," Oda said. The anger
she'd been suppressing surged into her throat, lacing through

her words. "Our family shouldn't be splintered. We shouldn't have been put in a position to deceive Artur."

"He deceived first," Cynda retorted, squeezing her hands. "Remember that, and remember that whatever happens, you will never be my enemy."

Cynda gave Oda a final embrace, then disappeared into the secret passageway, where she would wait for Iva to join her.

The room was silent then, save for the fire crackling in the hearth. Oda stood before it, wrapping her arms around her middle, a deep sense of discomfort creeping over her. Although the fabric Cynda had draped her in was beautiful, she would never feel like *Oda* in a gown.

But then Thorne emerged from the bathing chamber and spied her wearing it. When his lips parted in surprise and his cheeks stained red, Oda smiled.

"I was just thinking how awkward I feel wearing this," she said, smoothing her skirts as she approached him. "But perhaps I can make an exception from time to time."

"You won't feel so awkward when I free you of it," Thorne said with a wicked grin.

He closed the distance between them, bending to kiss her. Oda rose on her tiptoes to better meet him, grasping the lapels of his tunic to pull him closer. She had not anticipated kissing Thorne again, much less being *ordered* into a marriage bond with him. It was all more than she had believed possible.

"How is this real?" she whispered in wonder.

Thorne nipped at her lower lip. "We owe Iva a debt," he replied, heavy-lidded and breathless. "This is her doing."

Oda tucked his still-damp hair behind his ears. "Have you ever defied so many orders in your lifetime?"

His laugh was a pleasant rumble as he moved to kiss her jaw. She shivered as he whispered, "Never. But I told you—you are worth everything, and I would do it all again."

Thorne pressed a trail of slow, deliberate kisses down the

side of her throat. Oda went pliant against him, gripping his tunic in her fists as her lashes fluttered shut. Then he returned to her mouth, cradling her face in his hands as he deepened the kiss.

They lost themselves like that for a little while, standing before the fire and the runestone altar. When they heard the key turn in the chamber door, they broke apart, but Thorne captured Oda's hands and kissed her fingers, holding her close.

"Are you sure you want this?" Thorne whispered.

Oda swallowed hard. "If I had my choice, I would love you in the open—no need for secrets or deceit. But if this is the only way we can be together, then yes. I'm sure."

"It will be a heavy secret to carry," said Thorne.

"I know." Oda smoothed his tunic, craning her neck to look him in the eye. "But we'll carry it together."

When they heard the light swish of Iva's skirts and the door closing softly, they turned to greet her, hand in hand. She held several long strands of gold ribbon, and her cheeks were pink with exertion. The excitement in her expression was apparent, and Oda's heart surged with joy.

"Artur sleeps." Iva smiled warmly. "Are you ready to begin?"

Thorne tightened his grip on Oda's hand, then cast his silencing spell. "Yes," he said, his voice warm and rich.

Iva led the way to the altar, where she draped the golden ribbons. "As I understand it, my only role is to provide you with the word. Clan Beran's magic will work on my behalf." She motioned them forward. "Stand side by side before the altar."

They took their places, facing Iva.

"Now, Thorne," Iva instructed, "place your left palm in the center of the runestone, over the ribbons."

Thorne did so. He looped his right arm around the small of Oda's back.

"And Oda, place your left hand over his."

Once Oda had done as instructed, Iva began to drape the

golden threads up and over their hands, binding them atop the stone. Oda could feel Thorne's gaze trained on her, and she looked up to meet his eyes. As Iva worked, he leaned down to brush a kiss against her mouth.

Iva smiled softly, blushing. "I was right about you, and I'm glad of it. Who could have guessed we would have this chance?"

"We're indebted," Oda replied. "Thank you."

"When you find someone you can truly love in spite of all the obstacles ahead," Iva said as she tied the lengths of ribbon into a loose but intricate knot that rested atop Oda's hand, "that is the person you should hold close."

She pressed a hand over her heart and closed her eyes.

"Now, as Artur by proxy, I grant you a secret word that only the two of you will share as husband and wife. It's a term of endearment, imbued with the magic of the overlord's throne. When applied to vows of your own making, the word will bind you and etch your rune into the stone, forever immortalizing you in Clan Beran's lineage of rulers."

"So we create our own vows?" Thorne asked, his brow creased with concern.

"As I understand, yes," Iva answered with a nod. "You make your promises to one another, incorporating the term. Are you ready?"

Thorne's throat bobbed, and Oda bit back a smile at his hesitancy. She conjured a small orb of healing magic in her right hand, offering it to him. When she pressed her palm to his chest, he sighed with relief.

"Yes," he finally answered.

"Very well," said Iva. "Your word is *sjovyn*. It means 'bound by vow.' Use it well and share it with no one. When you're ready, you may say your vows; either of you can begin."

Oda reached up to stroke his cheek. "I'll start," she said softly. "Thorne, my *sjovyn*, I swear to love you, to laugh with you, to lead alongside you in whatever way you ask. In times of sadness, I will hold your heart, and in times of joy, I will delight in it."

Thorne fixed his warm gaze on her. He grasped her hand, turning his head to kiss her palm. "If I try to give you beautiful words, I'll be a disappointment."

Oda laughed softly before Thorne continued.

"I always believed my strength would earn me the love I was seeking. But the one who saw me at my weakest was the one who loved me most. *Sjovyn*, Oda, I want to be by your side until my days come to an end."

He leaned down to brush a gentle, reverent kiss to her lips.

Beneath their hands, the runestone began to glow brighter. The runes blazed to life, their dull white converging into a piercing beam. Then, the stone itself heated as though ignited from the inside, shining with the same hue as the runes.

Thorne gasped as a pulse of white power wound its way up his arm, then encircled his body before wrapping itself around Oda, too. She watched that magic fill his eyes, and for a moment, they glowed white, too.

As quickly as it happened, it was over, and he was staring at her wide-eyed, his irises bright with the rush of power.

Then, the gold ribbons that bound their hands shimmered to life, the same color as the healing magic they shared. Oda watched the ribbons tighten around their hands, then burst into gold dust, which scattered over their joined hands and sank into their skin.

When she turned her hand over, a golden rune shone on her wrist. Thorne held out his wrist, showing her his own matching mark. And on the surface of the stone, where their joined hands had rested a moment before, that same rune had been etched in shining white magic.

"It's complete," Iva whispered, an awestruck expression on her wide-eyed face. "Beautiful."

Iva didn't linger, but instead left Oda and Thorne alone together, slipping through the hidden exit in search of Cynda.

Thorne wasted no time in scooping Oda up where she stood. In a few long strides, he carried her to the bed on the room's far side. She cried out, laughing as he lay her on the soft mattress covered in silks and furs.

Bracing his body over hers, Thorne brushed kisses over her forehead. Her eyelids. Her cheeks. Her nose. Her mouth.

She wrapped her arms around him and knocked him off balance, bringing him down to lie beside her. He grinned, turning onto his side and studying the rune on his inner wrist. Already, the gold marking was beginning to fade, as was Oda's.

"It must be a trick of the magic," she mused, reaching up to unlace the collar of Thorne's tunic. "Secret marriage; secret rune."

"Mmm," Thorne hummed, leaning in to kiss her again.

He ran his fingertips along her back, studying the lacing of her gown until he found the knot Cynda had tied at the base of her spine. As he began to work it loose, he said, "The best part of the secret is keeping you near."

"How will we manage all this?" she asked, sitting up and turning her back to give him better access to the ribbons.

"With the secrecy of rulers," he answered, tugging at the ribbons to loosen them, "and the strategy of warriors."

"Skills we should hone regardless," Oda said softly, closing her eyes as Thorne slid his warm palm over her bare back.

Carefully, he helped her work her way out of the gown, pressing kisses to every inch of skin he exposed. Oda wasn't quite so patient with his garments; she ripped the seams of his tunic in trying to help him remove it.

Thorne only laughed, then guided her back down to lie with him.

With the morning's dread long behind them, the night passed in unhurried bliss. Oda knew the quiet moments they spent together might be seldom, and nights like this one few and far between, but she would cherish every moment they were given and savor every second they stole.

Late into the night, as the moon shone down through the skylight, Thorne gathered Oda close and whispered, "Did you see him, too?" he asked. "Or did I imagine it?"

Oda raised her head from the spot on his shoulder where she'd been lying. "Who? When?"

He shook his head, then ran a hand over his face before he said, "Berav. He appeared to me during the rite. It was so bright; I couldn't look for long."

"When your eyes went white," Oda murmured, pushing up onto her elbow to study him. "Then he's not dead?"

"Not dead," Thorne confirmed, reaching up to trace his fingertips over the shell of her ear. "I... he said nothing, but it seemed as though he had been waiting for that moment. For us."

"So he didn't break his silence," she mused, "but he came to you."

Thorne stroked her cheek. "I believe he did."

Had they truly received Berav's blessing during the binding rite? Oda wasn't sure, but the look of wonder in Thorne's eyes was enough to buoy her. The obstacles that loomed ahead would not be easy to navigate, but if Clan Beran's silent god was on their side, perhaps there was hope for a happy future.

CHAPTER 31

THORNE

The next afternoon, Thorne, Iva, a small contingent of Beravakt, and the remaining sentries stood just outside Fortress Halgeir's gates, bidding farewell to the young women from the selection. A small boat was docked on the shore, and the women had climbed inside together. No one spoke, and the mood was somber. The only sound in the cavernous gorge was the gentle lapping of the river against the shore.

Warm sun shone down on them, and the sky overhead was a rich, clear blue. Thorne was glad for the brilliant splash of color today—the flowing water glinting in the sun, the gorge's clay-colored walls rising all around them, and the colorful array of smooth stones and pebbles covering the shore. He took a deep, steadying breath and clasped his hands behind his back. The women's families had been allowed to say their goodbyes back in the fortress, but only Clan Beran's leaders and defenders were permitted to step out to the water's edge today. Artur was reportedly still ill and sleeping heavily in his chamber, so he had been left to recover.

Rynd and Mjit had been tasked with rowing the boat down-river, then traveling with the women to an undisclosed location.

From what Thorne understood, Cynda and the others would live together wherever they settled, and the clan would provide for them for the duration of the five years. Artur's discreet contacts throughout Rodhlan would be tasked with looking in on them from time to time to ensure all was well.

"*To make sure they stay put*," Oda had grumbled early that morning.

That was true. He and Oda both had misgivings about this long separation on the families' behalf. Still, the tradition would have continued as long as Artur ruled, regardless of who Thorne had married. So they had tried their best to make peace with it, and focused on enjoying one another fully while they'd had the chance.

In all his years of working toward this moment, Thorne had never imagined himself in love, much less happy with the person he'd chosen. He had rarely taken the time to consider what he might want, or what might be possible for him, until Oda. Now, though, he'd begun to envision what their future might look like with her by his side.

Still, his fear of being discovered was already at odds with the hope that bloomed in his heart. First, they would have to decide how to navigate the next five years.

Between now and then, they would focus on gathering more information about Artur's network in Rodhlan. There may yet be a way for Thorne to protect himself, his wife, and Iva without being forced to live in secrecy forever.

From his post by the tall stone gate, he snuck a glance in Oda's direction. As though anticipating it, her green eyes flicked toward him, and a faint smile played across her lips before she refocused on the boat once more.

And this was how it would be, for now. They would play

their roles before the clan, but behind closed doors, they would be Thorne and Oda—husband and wife. She would be his *sjovyn*, and they would focus on each day as it came until the path forward was clear.

EPILOGUE
ODA

Six Months Later

Oda worked quietly in the chamber she shared with her mother, gathering her belongings for travel. Elda sat by in terse silence, watching her daughter warily. Her once jovial expression was drawn, and deep frown lines had formed on either side of her mouth.

Elda drew a fur shawl around her shoulders, gripped it tightly, and shivered. The lavender tunic and gray skirt she wore had not proven warm enough to ward off today's chill. She had wound her long braids into a tight bun at the nape of her neck.

"Did I tell you that you look pretty today, Mum?" Oda asked tentatively. She had always loved the contrast of lavender fabric against her mother's dark skin.

Her mother sighed but didn't respond right away. It had pained Oda to watch Elda grieve Cynda's departure. Now, she was inflicting a wound of her own.

"I still don't understand why you must leave me, too," Elda lamented quietly as Oda moved about the small space. She pressed a hand against her cheek and sighed heavily. "Have I not endured enough, losing *one* of my daughters?"

"You're not losing me, Mum," Oda replied calmly. "I told you; I'm feeling restless here, and I want to see Rune. I can help him regain his strength—get him sailing again."

"He can get along just fine without you."

Oda sighed and shook her head.

Nothing had been the same since Elda's return the month prior. She had brought good news of Rune's improvement but had been met with devastation when she'd discovered Cynda's absence. Elda had flown into a fury, demanding to see the overlord herself. It had taken Oda, Thorne, and Iva to calm and deter her. Ever since, Elda had held a grudge against Oda for refusing to intervene.

Although Oda had been tempted to give Elda the full story, she couldn't. It was best not to implicate her mother by pulling her too far into the fray. Their deception had already yielded more unanticipated results than they'd bargained for, and she wasn't ready to deepen the pit any further.

For now, Oda allowed Elda to assume that she knew nothing of *who* had been chosen for Thorne, just like the rest of the clan.

There was a soft tapping at the chamber door, and Oda opened it to find Iva standing outside. Today, she was dressed in a fitted tunic of brown and gold, gray leggings, and a warm, fur-lined vest. Her curls had been plaited into a thick braid she had draped over one shoulder, and her lips were tinged glossy pink.

She flashed Oda a broad smile. "Ljós is waiting for you."

Oda hefted her traveling satchel and crossed the room to Elda, kissing her on the cheek. When her mother stiffened at her touch, her heart sank.

"I'll return soon." Oda stepped over the threshold and out into the cool autumn air. "I promise."

"You'll weather the winter on the coast; mark my words," Elda argued. "This is why I wanted you with me last spring. No worries of ice or snow, or of trials and daughters sent away."

"I know, Mum." She craned her neck, attempting to make eye contact with Elda before shutting the chamber door. When her mother didn't answer, she said, "I love you," then closed the door with a soft click.

Walking away was a blessed relief. Oda wanted to make everything better for Elda—for everyone—but that was impossible.

"Give me that satchel," Iva demanded when they were out of earshot. "And do you need to take *so* many weapons?"

Oda scowled, checking over her shoulders to ensure she had indeed donned both her broadsword and her axe. *So many weapons.* "It's *fine*. We've made it this long without a fuss; don't start now."

"I can't believe you've waited so long to leave," Iva countered.

"Would you have done any differently, were you in my position?" Oda asked.

Iva smiled. "No. I would have stolen as much time with him as I could."

With a grin, Oda replied, "Then we have an understanding."

Ljós had returned to Fortress Halgeir with Elda last month. Today's planned departure for Iathium was a blessing; the healer had agreed to take Oda all the way to the western coast before doubling back and heading for the city. The Rí was in excellent health, he'd said, and it would be no trouble to take a brief detour.

They arrived at Ljós's chambers a little while later, where Iva again insisted that Oda offload her bag, if nothing else.

Oda grudgingly obliged, setting her satchel on one of the healer's sturdy worktables and lowering herself carefully onto a stool. She exhaled, then focused on controlling her breathing. After a moment, each breath came easier than the next.

Iva stood before Oda, studying her carefully. "You're sure about the coast?" she asked, reaching out to adjust the fur-lined traveling cloak Oda had draped herself in. Beneath it, she wore a loose, soft tunic of red wool and comfortable brown trousers. "My daughter would welcome you in the city if we asked."

"Too conspicuous," Oda said. "Visiting my uncle offers the best explanation. We're lucky Artur agreed to it at all, after everything that's happened."

They were lucky Iva was so persuasive. Artur was completely taken by her, and that fact alone had likely saved their necks.

"You're probably right," Iva said. "Remember, you and Thorne will only have a few moments to spare. Ljós is already on his way to the boat."

The chamber door opened behind her, and she leaned in for an embrace. "He's here," she whispered, pressing a kiss to Oda's cheek. "Safe travels; I'll see you when you return."

Iva swept from the room as Thorne stepped inside, his warm eyes scanning Oda protectively. He was dressed in leather trousers and a heavy brown tunic, and his blond hair was pulled away from his face. His cheeks were ruddy from the harsh, cold wind, and she wondered if he had spent the early morning hours training outside his chamber as he preferred to.

Thorne locked the door and silenced the chamber, then crossed to Oda in a few long strides. She rose to meet his kiss as he gathered her close.

"*Sjovyn*," Thorne whispered, the low timbre of his voice washing over her.

Oda wrapped her arms around his neck, rising on her tiptoes to give him better access. "I worried I might not see you today," she admitted, brushing the tip of her nose against his.

"*That* wasn't going to happen." He cupped her cheek and kissed her forehead. "How are you feeling?"

She grimaced. "I have never worried so much in my life. I don't think that's going to improve."

"Being worried is *my* job." Thorne pressed his lips to hers again. His warm palm drifted to her softly rounded belly, only just becoming visible, and rested there. He bent his head to look into her eyes, his gaze searching. "You'll be out of my sight for so *long*."

Oda wrapped her arm around him and rested her cheek on his chest. They stilled together, waiting for the child in her womb to kick. This was the last time Thorne would be near his child before Oda gave birth. After that, they were unsure when he would meet his firstborn face-to-face, if the chance ever presented itself at all.

Her heart ached for him—for all three of them. These past months of secrecy and uncertainty had been sweetened by Thorne's attentiveness. He had taken the liberty of caring for Oda himself, using his healing abilities to soothe her nausea in the early days, assess her progress, and see to the baby's wellbeing. She could sense the bond that had already formed between Thorne and their child, and the thought of separating this way was almost unbearable.

The baby wiggled just beneath Oda's ribs. She gasped lightly, grabbing Thorne's hand and chasing the movement. When the child shifted again, bumping against his palm, he closed his eyes, a sad smile playing across his lips.

"I'll miss this," he said, "and I'll miss you."

"I'll return as soon as I can," Oda swore, her tender eyes meeting his.

It would be easy enough to become stranded on the coast with her family in winter, but when spring came, Artur would expect her back.

Between now and then, Oda was counting on birthing their

baby and determining her next steps. She'd considered asking Rune or one of her Énna cousins for help with raising the child, but discerning who to trust with her secret would require caution.

Regardless, no one could know the identity of the babe's father.

"I wish to be there for the birth," Thorne murmured for the thousandth time. No matter how many times they'd talked about this, hearing the heartache in his voice never became easier. "You should not have to do this alone. It isn't right."

"If you could be with me, you would be," Oda replied with a sigh. "I know that without a doubt, but I'll wish for you every moment."

Thorne wrapped Oda in a comforting embrace, and for a long moment, they simply held one another in the healer's chamber.

If all went according to plan, Oda would return in a few short months, and they would resume their ruse. Their child would be safe on the other side of the continent, far away from Fortress Halgeir. Although the decision was heartbreaking for them both, this was the right path forward.

For now.

There was no choice but to stay on course and follow through with their plans. At least until they could find reasonable recourse for their deception, if that even existed at all.

It had been folly to overlook the possibility of pregnancy, especially so soon after they'd wed. But here they were, forced to play their roles. Leading a separate life in secret. And now, they were bringing a child into the world who they might never get the chance to know.

Who might never truly know them.

Oda heaved a sigh, tightening her arms around Thorne. He released her long enough to kneel and grasp her hand, pressing a soft kiss to her belly. When he rose again, he cupped her face in his large, gentle hands.

Time was running out; they had lingered here too long.

"I'll keep trying to find a way to be there for you," he said. "I swear."

Whether he succeeded or not, she knew his heart, and she knew he would be with her no matter how many miles separated them.

Oda coaxed him down for one last kiss. "And I love you for that," she replied.

~

THE END

NOTES & ACKNOWLEDGEMENTS

To say that Thorne and Oda hold my entire heart is an understatement.

Ruse of Heirs has lived in my mind and heart for over two years now, and I'm so excited to finally be able to share it.

This book began as a short detour from the *Sovereign of Clans* production process. I saw it as essential writing before we dive into Thorne and Oda's POVs in *Sovereign*. Originally, I intended for it to be a novella. But it grew well beyond that, as stories often do.

From a contextual standpoint, writing *Ruse* allowed me to give plenty of breathing room to a backstory I'd first attempted to write into *Vow of Magic*, then removed. Rather than skimming the high points in one of the larger novels, it became increasingly important to give this story the attention it deserved.

As a "discovery writer," I don't always know where my narratives (or characters) are going before I sit down to write. Their stories unfold alongside the greater narrative. Thorne's character has been with me since the first draft of *Defender of Histories*, although he doesn't make an appearance in the series until book 2 (*Keeper of Keys*). Oda emerged during *Keeper*, and their story has grown as the story progresses.

When their relationship and backstory emerged, it was clear we'd need to journey down that path together.

If you've made it this far, thank you for being part of my journey and for embracing my characters and stories.

To Elyse Grothendick, Tim O'Hearn, and Marcella W., thank you for reading and re-reading my early drafts. Your feedback and reactions to the story not only helped me strengthen my writing; they also kept me going.

Elyse, you helped make this publication possible in the middle of a challenging time, and I so appreciate your willingness to dive in and help me push this book baby over the finish line.

To the friends, family, colleagues, and mentors who have supported me on this journey: I'm so grateful to each of you.

I love you all. On to the next story!

- Haley

GO BACK TO WHERE IT ALL BEGAN...

DEFENDER OF HISTORIES

HALEY WALDEN

THE WITNESS TREE CHRONICLES

I

DEFENDER OF HISTORIES
THE WITNESS TREE CHRONICLES, BOOK 1

When truth threatens power, the victor controls the pen.

Unpredictable and heart-pounding, enjoy this gripping epic fantasy with magic, political intrigue, tragic romance, and lovable, flawed heroes.

Bookish scholar Lira has dedicated her life to studying and preserving her kingdom's histories. When the charming young king, Eremon, chooses her to inherit the royal archive, she can hardly believe her luck.

But those who control the throne have secretly dominated the population by stealing their rightful magic. And when Lira inherits forbidden magic, she quickly becomes a target.

As Lira's bond with the king deepens, a terrifying truth emerges: dark magic is rising, and no one can be trusted - not even her friend and protector, Aidryn, who begs her to leave Eremon and the city behind.

When Lira finds herself alone, with enemies at every turn, will she have the courage to embrace her true power and fight the dark magic that threatens her world?

Defender of Histories is the spellbinding first installment of the epic fantasy series, *The Witness Tree Chronicles*.

"It has everything you'd want from a story: fast-paced adventure, ancient libraries and general book nerdery, a slow-

burn friends to lovers romance... be still my beating heart."
★★★★★

"This was a book that made me drop everything going on in my adult life until I finished." ★★★★★

Want more? Find *Defender of Histories* (*The Witness Tree Chronicles, Book 1*) at your favorite online book retailer.

Learn more:
authorhaleywalden.com

THANK YOU!

Enjoyed what you read? Please leave a review on Goodreads or the retailer of your choice. Reviews help readers like you discover new stories, characters, and worlds they'll love.

(Besides, Thorne says his story is just as important as the *boy-king's*, so it needs plenty of eyes on it so readers can pick a favorite already. IYKYK.)

About the Author

Haley Walden writes fast-paced, character-driven epic fantasy with magical adventures, spellbinding love stories, and unforgettable friendships. As a multi-passionate geek she has many obsessions, including music, martial arts, history, pop culture, and musical theatre. She lives in Alabama with her husband and children.

www.authorhaleywalden.com

LET'S KEEP IN TOUCH!

Stay up-to-date on bookish news and happenings:
www.authorhaleywalden.com

Follow me on Instagram, TikTok, and Facebook:
@authorhaleywalden